"Hurry, Ben!" Jake shrieked.
"Swim! He's after you!"

"Swim, Ben! Swim!" Jake screamed.

The log was closer now.

Only it wasn't a log!

It wasn't covered with bark. It was covered with thick, big, warty-looking scales. There were two yellow-green eyes. Two round nostrils. And at the very front of the log, there were teeth— white, shining fangs. . . .

Alligator!

The word screamed inside my head. And at that very second, I heard myself screaming, just like Jake was screaming: *"Swim, Ben! Swim!"*

Books by Bill Wallace

A Dog Called Kitty
Red Dog
Trapped in Death Cave

Available from Archway Paperbacks

Beauty
Danger on Panther Peak
    (original title: *Shadow on the Snow*)
Danger in Quicksand Swamp
Ferret in the Bedroom, Lizards in the Fridge
Snot Stew

Available from MINSTREL Books

DANGER IN QUICKSAND SWAMP

BILL WALLACE

A MINSTREL® BOOK

PUBLISHED BY POCKET BOOKS

New York   London   Toronto   Sydney   Tokyo   Singapore

This book is a work of fiction. Names, characters, places and incidents
are either the product of the author's imagination or are used fictitiously.
Any resemblance to actual events or locales or persons, living or dead,
is entirely coincidental.

 A Minstrel Book published by
POCKET BOOKS, a division of Simon & Schuster Inc.
1230 Avenue of the Americas, New York, NY 10020

Copyright © 1989 by Bill Wallace
Cover artwork copyright © 1991 by Bryce Lee

ISBN: 0-671-75424-6

First Minstrel Books printing August 1991

10 9 8 7 6 5 4 3 2 1

A MINSTREL BOOK and colophon are registered trademarks
of Simon & Schuster Inc.

Printed in the U.S.A.

To MARGERY, for her patience and persistence,
and to the understanding people in The Coffee Shop
at the Stamford Town Center in Connecticut

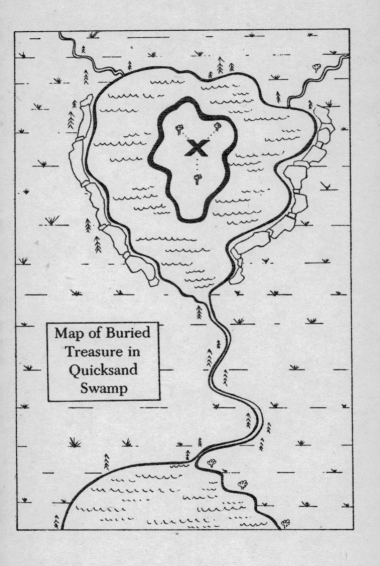

Map of Buried
Treasure in
Quicksand
Swamp

DANGER IN QUICKSAND SWAMP

CHAPTER 1

" 'It was a hot, dry summer, just like this one, when Robert disappeared,' Mr. Grissam told me. Then, after he said that, he just got up and walked away."

A cloud of dust belched up behind the school bus as it pulled away. Jake and I scurried up the long road, trying to stay out of the swirling dirt until it had a chance to settle. When we had gone far enough, we began to slow our pace.

"That's all?" Jake asked. "Mr. Grissam just got up and walked off?"

I nodded.

Jake kicked at a pile of dust beneath a bent-over sunflower. "What do you reckon Mr. Grissam meant?" Jake asked.

I shook my head. "No idea."

"Did you even ask about the loan?"

"Yep."

"You tell him what it was for?"

"Yep."

"And he just walked off?"

I tucked my backpack under my right arm and put my left hand on my hip.

" 'It was a hot, dry summer, just like this one, when Robert disappeared.' That's what Ol' Man Grissam said."

Jake shook his head. "He's weird!"

"Yeah," I agreed. "I mean, he's the richest man in the whole town, but he always wears that same gray suit with the little stripes running down it."

"Yeah," Jake said, "and those same baggy pants."

I shrugged. "I bet he's got a bunch of suits. They just all look the same."

Jake nodded. "And he always wears a red tie and those fancy boots. Daddy told me they were real, honest-to-goodness alligator boots. There isn't anybody else in the county who can afford alligator boots. He's got all that money and he won't even lend us enough to fix our lawn mowers."

Jake shook his head. "He's weird," he repeated. Then he looked back over his shoulder. "His kid's weird, too."

I glanced behind us. Tiffany Grissam was walking with Lisa. They'd whisper and giggle, then walk a ways and whisper and giggle some more.

My mouth twisted up to one side as I looked at Jake. "Why's she weird?"

"It's just . . . well . . . she never does anything with the rest of us," said Jake. "She doesn't play basketball or softball with the girls. She doesn't do stuff with us after school. She never spends the night at a friend's house, 'cause she's always with her mom or dad or that lady who lives with them."

"Maybe it isn't her fault." I motioned up the road.

A young woman stood at the end of a long, cement driveway. She leaned against the brick pillar that supported a huge steel gate. A hand shielded her eyes from the glare of the afternoon sun.

Her name was Elizabeth. She was the Grissam's "au pair," which is a fancy French word for baby-sitter. Only, Elizabeth wasn't French. She came from England. Ol' Man Grissam brought her to America to take care of Tiffany. To anyone else in Broken Bow, she'd be called a baby-sitter. But since she took care of the banker's kid, she was an au pair.

"Maybe it isn't her fault," I repeated. "Maybe Tiffany would like to play with us or spend more time with her friends. Maybe her dad just won't let her do anything without a grown-up around."

I jerked my head at the old, crinkled poster on the telephone pole. There was a picture of a boy, although it was so weather-worn you could barely make it out. Above the picture, in big letters, it said:

> ROBERT GRISSAM
> Age 15
> Missing
> August 11, 1985
> Last seen wearing blue jeans,
> plaid shirt, and running shoes
> LARGE REWARD
> for information

"If somebody in your family disappeared, wouldn't you want a guard for the others?" I said, holding my hands up. When I did, the empty backpack fell from under my arm. I bent down to get it, knowing we would have to wait here for Lisa to catch up, anyway.

"See you," Tiffany called as she headed up her branch of the road.

Jake, Lisa, and I took the branch to the right. It was a dirt road like the one we were just on. Lisa lagged behind. Jake and I walked slow, so she wouldn't have to struggle to keep up.

It was a pretty day—still hot, like usual for the last week in May. I couldn't ever remember it being so dry, though. The road was more dust than dirt. The leaves on the trees drooped and curled in the heat. The ones on the lower branches were so covered with dust, they didn't even look like leaves. Even the grass along the side of the road was brown and dead-looking. And like everything else, it was covered with dust.

Jake nudged me with an elbow. "Did you ask Ol' Man Grissam's brother about the loan? Kenny's a lot friendlier and nicer than his brother. Not as nutty-acting, either."

I shook my head. "No, he wasn't there. Besides, my dad doesn't care much for him."

There was a gap beside us where we could see the river through the trees. Well, we really couldn't see the river because it was so low, but we could see the banks.

"We going out plug hunting this afternoon?" Jake asked. Only, I didn't hear him. I was thinking about Mr. Grissam again.

"You know," I said, "it was silly to ask Mr. Grissam for a loan to fix our lawn mowers. School's just out and we've got plenty of time to work, but the grass is brown and dead as a doornail. You can't mow dead grass." I looked Jake square in the eye. "Asking for a loan to fix our lawn mowers was *dumb*! We're gonna have to figure out another way to earn money to buy our fishing boat."

Jake cocked his head to the side.

"What's that got to do with plug hunting?"

"Huh?" I frowned.

"Plug hunting," Jake repeated. "You want to go down to the river and hunt for fishing plugs today?"

"Oh." I shook my head. "Not today. Grandma has some ceramic stuff she's gonna take to get fired tomorrow. She wants me to help her with it. Maybe Sunday."

We stopped where the road forked off to Jake's house. His drive was a winding little road, but through the pines I could see the white, frame house far back in the forest. He waited with me until Lisa caught up. Then, punching me on the shoulder, he said, "See you in the morning."

Lisa waddled along beside me. She was a little plump and always slow and poky. Her being so slow and messing with my things were the worst part about having a little sister. We walked in silence for a long time. The only sounds were the dry pine needles rustling with the push of a gentle breeze.

I offered to carry the stuff she was bringing home from the last day of school, but Lisa clung to all the junk in her arms.

"You looking forward to fourth grade next year?" I asked.

Lisa didn't answer. We walked across the low-water bridge. It was a big slab of concrete that was usually covered with water that flowed into the river. Only now, it was dry and covered with dust.

"I like Tiffany," Lisa said.

I nodded. "She seems nice."

"I wonder why her mama and daddy won't let her come over and play."

"Maybe they're afraid that if they let her out of their sight, she'll disappear like Robert. Or, maybe they figure they're too good for poor folks like us." I shrugged.

Lisa's bottom lip stuck out.

"Tiffany doesn't feel that way. She's nice. I like her."

When we got over the crest of the hill to where we could see the house, the first thing I noticed was the truck.

Daddy drove log trucks. There were always a couple of flatbeds around, usually loaded with pine logs on their way to the mill. There was an old cab parked beside the work shed that Daddy had been trying to fix up. This truck was different from the ones that were usually parked around our place. It was shorter than a log truck and had side rails all around it. The whole thing was covered with a green tarp.

I trotted over to it. The flap in the back was loose, so I set my stuff down and climbed up to see what was there.

As I caught hold of the tarp, I thought I heard something move. Then another sound, like water sloshing.

Carefully, I lifted the tarp just a bit and saw a metal box. It was about five feet high and filled the whole bottom of the truck. The tarp was heavy, so I stuck my head and shoulders under it.

That's when I noticed the smell. My nose crinkled up, and I almost gagged.

Slowly, I pulled myself to where I could see over the edge of the box. It was dark under the tarp. I squinted, leaning forward.

Suddenly, there was a flash of movement. Right there in front of me, something long and shiny and slithery twisted and turned.

A leathery snout with warts on it rose up. A gaping mouth opened. Row after row of long, white teeth lunged toward my face.

I jerked back.

The jaws snapped shut.

I fell, sliding down from under the tarp and landing with a thud in the dust behind the truck. My bottom bounced so hard it sent stars shooting up through the top of my head.

"Dinosaur!" I gasped.

CHAPTER 2

For a second, my head spun. I tried to open my eyes, but they bobbed up and down around the bottom of my hair. I blinked a couple of times.

Daddy came running from the front door.

"Ben! Lisa! You two stay down off that truck," he called. "Ben? Ben, you all right?"

I blinked again. Finally, my eyes focused. I nodded. "I think so," I called back.

Lisa was beside me. She latched onto my arm, yanking like she was trying to help me up. Only, I didn't feel like getting up. I must have landed right on my tail-bone, since my seat hurt something terrible.

Shoving Lisa away, I yelled, "Run! Dinosaur."

Lisa took a step back. She cocked her head to the side, looking at me like I was *totally nuts*.

"Dinosaur?"

I pointed a finger at the truck. "Yes. In there. Get back."

Lisa just stood and shook her head. "Dinosaur," she repeated, almost giggling.

Daddy rushed over and knelt down beside me. "You okay, Ben?" He looked me over, then helped me to my feet. "You break anything? Where do you hurt?"

As gently as I could, I started brushing the dust off my bottom.

"I think I'm all right." Then, glancing up at the tarp, I remembered the white fangs on the monster that had snapped at me. "That thing . . . in the truck . . ." I took a step back. "It tried to bite . . . big . . . what . . . what . . . ?"

Lisa's giggles stopped my stammering. I looked at her. She held one hand over her mouth. The harder she tried to keep from laughing, the redder she got. Finally, she let her hand go and burst out: "Ben said it's a dinosaur," she laughed. Then to me: "Was it a *Tyrannosaurus rex* or a *Brontosaurus?*"

If Daddy hadn't been standing there, I would have popped her right in the mouth.

Daddy started dusting the seat of my britches.

"Ben's not that far off," he told Lisa. "I've got a truckload of alligators."

Lisa's mouth flopped open. I guess mine did, too, because neither one of us said a word. We only stood there, staring at Daddy. His smile seemed to stretch clear across his brown, weathered face.

"Really!" He motioned toward the truck. "Come on, I'll show you."

Neither of us moved.

Daddy walked over and started unhooking some of the big rubber trucker straps that held the tarp down. He climbed up on the back and threw the tarp over the wood rails so the rear of the truck was open. With a wave of his arm, he motioned to us.

"Come on. Take a look."

Lisa was the first to move. She walked over to Daddy. He took her hand to pull her up. "Don't hang onto the metal box. Hold onto the wood rail, instead. Them gators could snap a hand off quicker than you could blink an eye."

Lisa stretched up on her tiptoes and leaned over the big metal box.

"Ooohhh. Yuck!"

Daddy laughed when she grabbed her nose and pinched.

"They have a smell to them, don't they?" he chuckled. Then he turned to look at me. "Come on, Ben. Come take a look."

I remembered that scaly snout and the sharp, white fangs that snapped shut only inches from my face—and I didn't know whether I wanted to take a look or not. I figured I'd seen just about enough.

Daddy waved again, and I started toward him. He reached down a big, rough, calloused hand and helped me up. I held onto the wood rail of the truck like he had told Lisa to. Ever so slowly, I stretched on my toes and peered over the edge of the metal crate.

Any second, I expected those white fangs to come snapping at my nose. But with the three of us standing there, the alligators started moving to the far end of the container.

There must have been a hundred of the slimy things in there. They climbed and slithered over one another. They curled and wriggled and splashed the yucky brown-green water. Every now and then, one would get mad when another one stepped or crawled over him. Then the mad one would lunge at the other one and snap his huge jaws at him. It made a cracking sound like a gun going off.

I guess I'd been holding my breath, because when I finally sucked in air through my nose, the stench almost knocked me off the back of the truck.

"Oh, yuck," I said, fanning my face with a hand, "they stink!"

Daddy shrugged. "They've been in the crate since last night. It's a long drive from Louisiana to here in the hot sun. They're a little gamy, all right."

Despite the awful smell, we stood and watched the ugly creatures for a long time. At last, Daddy got hold of the tarp and started pulling it over the back of the truck.

"We got them stirred up enough. Best get down and close this thing so they can get some rest."

Lisa and I were so fascinated with the creepy things, we couldn't move. Daddy chuckled to himself as he pulled the tarp right over us. Being left there in the dark with those slimy, nasty things wasn't that much fun, so we crawled out from under the tarp and got down.

"What are you doing with a truckload of alligators?" I asked. "You drive a log truck."

Daddy shrugged. "Got a four-day vacation and needed the money. David Parker, the game ranger at Broken Bow, called and said the State Department of Wildlife Management needed somebody to haul a load of alligators in from Louisiana. Asked if I wanted the job."

"Why are they hauling alligators in here?" Lisa asked.

"The wildlife department is restocking this area."

Lisa just stood there.

Daddy put a hand on both our shoulders and started walking us toward the house.

"This area of southeast Oklahoma used to be a native habitat for alligators. Back in the old days, there must have been quite a few around here. But when people started moving in, they killed them off. Alligator hides were worth a lot of money, even back then.

"The wildlife people are trying to put nature back to where it was before people came along and messed it up. I think it's a good idea, don't you?"

Lisa nodded. I shrugged. After seeing those jaws snap shut right in front of my face, I wasn't too crazy about having alligators *anyplace* around. I bet Jake would flip when he saw them, though.

After we got to the house, Lisa went to help Mama in the kitchen. I dropped my backpack on the couch and headed back outdoors.

"Where're you going?" Mama's voice came from the kitchen.

"Over to get Jake. I want him to see the alligators."

Mama peeked around the doorjamb. "I've got supper ready."

"I'll eat after I show Jake."

"Supper first, then you can go to Jake's."

"But, Mama . . ."

"Eat first."

"Mama . . ."

Shoot! It was the first time anything exciting had happened all year, and I had to eat before I could tell anybody about it.

CHAPTER 3

When I raced out on the front porch after dinner, I heard the screen go *bang* behind me. I cringed, waiting for Daddy to yell at me. When he didn't, I charged down the steps.

Then . . . *kersplat* . . . I crashed right into Jake.

We must have both been traveling at a pretty good speed, since the collision knocked the wind out of me and sent Jake tumbling backward into the front yard.

I sucked in a deep breath, trying to get my wind back. Jake scampered to his feet and dusted himself off. Then at the same instant, we both shouted:

"Come on, I've got something to show you. . . ."

We each stopped, realizing we were saying the exact same thing at the exact same time. We kind of shook our heads and frowned.

Then I went to help Jake dust himself off.

"You're not gonna believe what Daddy's got in his truck."

"You're not gonna believe what I found on the river."

I put my hands on my hips.

"What I've got to show *you* is important."

Jake put his hands on his hips.

"What I've got to show *you* is important."

I pointed to the truck.

"I gotta show you first. The truck's right here."

Jake shook his head.

"I gotta show you first. What I found is about a mile down the river, and if we don't leave now, it's gonna be dark."

I stuck my bottom lip out and shot a breath of air up my forehead. Jake stood there, glaring at me. I turned around and glanced toward the west. The sun was already down. There was kind of a golden glow in the sky. It was still light, but it wouldn't be for long.

"We can't walk a mile and back before dark," I told him. "Let me show you what Daddy brought home, then first thing in the morning, we can go see what you found."

Jake stood real stiff for a minute. Then his shoulders sagged and he smiled.

"Okay. But yours better be good."

Jake jumped almost as high as I did when he saw the alligators, only he didn't fall off the truck. I laughed when he grabbed his nose and acted like he was going to throw up from the stink.

Even though alligators were ugly things, they sure were interesting to watch. We stood there, hanging onto the back of the truck until it was too dark even to see them. I went and got my flashlight to lend Jake so he could get home.

In our part of Oklahoma, you don't go tromping through the woods after dark. Not without a good light. There are too many snakes around. Long before I'd ever heard about poisonous snakes in science class, Daddy had told me that all four kinds in North America live around here. We have rattlesnakes, copperheads, water moccasins, and the little black, yellow, and red-striped coral snakes that are most deadly of all. It was mostly because of the copperheads and the moccasins that Jake needed the light. There were a lot of them.

He'd get it back to me first thing tomorrow. My only problem was making sure I was awake when he came.

*   *   *

The next morning I woke up to a loud *whomp* sound and felt my head bounce. Before I could even blink, Jake was on my bed bopping me with my pillow.

I covered my head with my arms. Jake hit me again on the side, so I kicked the covers back and got up.

"Quit!"

"Get up. We gotta get goin'. You gonna sleep your whole life away?"

I yawned so wide that my ears crackled. "I'm up, I'm up."

"Well, don't just stand there yawning. Get dressed. Let's get goin'."

I blinked and rubbed the sleep out of my eyes. "It's Saturday. Don't you ever sleep late?"

Jake was standing with my pillow in his hand. His grin stretched from ear to ear.

"Not when there's something as important as what I have to show you. Now get moving or I'm gonna whomp you again."

He threatened with the pillow. I held my hand up, protecting myself. Jake put the pillow down and started making my bed while I looked around for my jeans and got clean socks and underpants out of the drawer.

Outside, Jake had leaned a shovel against the front porch. He grabbed it and held it across his chest like an army rifle.

"Ask your mom if you can take your shovel," he ordered.

My head tilted to the side. "Why? You find a buried treasure or somethin'?"

Jake shook his head. "Nope. Even better."

I knew Mama wouldn't mind if I took the shovel, so I didn't bother to ask. It was leaning against the hog-wire fence around the garden. Grandma kept the shovel there for digging up potatoes and carrots and stuff when they were ripe.

As we passed by the side of the house on the way to the river, I could hear Mama rattling around in the kitchen.

"Jake and I are goin' down on the river awhile," I called.

Mama's face appeared at the window. She waved her dish towel. "Okay. Watch for snakes. Be back in time for lunch."

I waved back to her. She always said "Watch for snakes."

A little path led to the river from the northwest corner of the hill where our house was. I followed Jake, watching for poison ivy.

At the bottom of the hill, the path split at a huge bald cypress tree. We took the left fork. The little path weaved and wound through stands of pin oak, cypress, and sweet gum whose thick, five-point leaves blocked out the sun.

I paused a second and looked at the river. Usually, it ran from the edge of the trees on our side, to the edge of the trees on the far bank. On a good day, I could barely throw a rock across it. Now, there was a whole bunch of sand on the banks and the river was no more than a narrow channel in the middle.

I must have stopped longer to stare at the water than I thought. When I looked back, Jake was far down the path. I had to jog to catch up with him.

"How much farther?"

He glanced over his shoulder. "Not far, now."

But we kept walking and walking and walking. "We almost there?"

"Just around the next bend."

We walked and walked and then walked some more.

There were places where the river would widen out. I tried to make pictures in my head, so I could remember where the wide spots, or holes, were. They would be good for fishing when the river came back up.

Finally, Jake left the path and walked out on the sandy bank that was once the riverbed. On a long, straight stretch of the bank, he stopped.

"It's right around here. I almost tripped over it when . . ."

His voice trailed off. He stood real still for a moment, looking at the sand. Finally, he looked up the bank, then down the bank, as he turned in a circle.

"It *was* here. . . ."

My shoulders sagged. All this walking and now he can't find what he was gonna show me, I told myself. That figures.

Jake looked at the trees. He looked at the way the river channel moved in a long, straight line. Then he looked back at the sand.

"I know it was here," he said. He started punching the sand with his shovel. "I know it was."

"What?" I asked.

Jake ignored me. I walked up behind him, careful to stay back a ways so he wouldn't stab my foot with his shovel.

"If you'll tell me what we're lookin' for, maybe I can help."

He just shook his head and kept jabbing the ground with his shovel.

I sat down in the sand and shook my head as I watched him running around like an idiot.

Another wild-goose chase, I told myself. Jake's always doing stuff like this.

CHAPTER 4

I was getting disgusted with Jake. The sand that he'd been punching with his shovel looked like the tracks of some monster who had been playing around on the bank.

With my hand, I smoothed the sand out over the little pictures I'd doodled with my finger. Jake had moved pretty far away, so I stood up and went after him. As I did, I glanced down at my shadow. There wasn't much shadow left. I'd learned to tell time at school, but I'd never had a watch. I did know that when my shadow disappeared, except by my feet, the sun was straight overhead. When that happened, it was twelve noon. It would take at least thirty minutes to walk back home, and Mama would be mad.

"Jake," I said when I caught up with him, "it's getting close to lunch. I'm gonna be in trouble with Mama if we don't get home."

He stabbed his shovel in the sand. "I know it's here, Ben, I promise." He rubbed his shoulder, which I guess was aching from raising his shovel up and down so much. "Five more minutes. Just five more."

I glanced at the shadow. It was getting awfully near to being gone. Five minutes would be cutting things pretty close, but . . .

"Okay," I answered, "five more, and that's it."

There was a small mound of sand on the bank about ten feet from where Jake was digging. It was right near the edge of the water. Maybe I could see a fish or something while I sat there, waiting.

I walked over, put my shovel in the sand, and plopped down on top of the mound. I didn't know what Jake was looking for, but I knew good and well that we weren't going to find it.

I crossed my legs, Indian-style, and started drawing a horse in the sand. Unlike the other sandy places where I'd been drawing, this stuff stuck to my finger. I wiped it on my jeans before I drew in the horse's tail and mane.

Right about then, I noticed my seat. All of a sudden, it felt cold, kind of like a car seat after somebody with a bathing suit has been sitting on it.

I got up to dust my bottom off. The sand *was* damp. It stuck to my pants and to my hands. I had to rub my hands together to get it off.

I frowned, squatting down and resting my arms on my knees. It didn't make sense. Everything else around here was dry as a bone, everything except this one little mound of sand. It just didn't figure.

Tilting my head, I dug my finger deep into the sand. It was damp all the way down. I could make a sand castle or a fort or something. I dug a little.

The sand was fine, but damp enough to work with. I started scooping out handfuls and smushing it together with my hands to make a wall.

After a while, I had built a good fort. It was about four feet square and the walls were pretty tall. All I needed to do now was build some barracks and a corral inside, then make lines up and down the walls with a stick so it looked like logs instead of sand.

The horse corral was almost finished when Jake walked up. I had gotten so carried away with my fort, I hadn't noticed how much time had slipped by. It must be past noon by now, and Mama would be really mad.

"I quit," he snapped. "I swear it was here, but I've looked all over and . . ."

When he stopped talking, I glanced up at him. Right in the middle of his sentence, his mouth flopped open and the words quit coming out. He stood there, frowning down at my fort.

"What are you doin'?" he asked.

"Building a fort."

"Where'd you get the sand?"

"Right here."

"Not out of the river?"

I shook my head. "Nope. Right here."

All of a sudden, Jake stepped on the front wall of my fort. His grungy, stinking tennis shoe flattened it. Then my lookout post toppled over.

Eyes tight, I glared at him.

"What are you . . ."

My eyes flashed when I saw the shovel coming down. I managed to yank my hand out of the way, just a second before the sharp blade sliced into the sand where I was digging. I jumped back.

He was on his knees in the middle of where my fort had been. He was digging in the sand like a puppy dog burying a bone. Sand was flying between his legs as he dug and dug.

"I told you it was here," he yelped. "I told you, didn't I? You were sittin' right on top of it."

My mouth curled up on one side. I shook my head. "You're nuts!"

"No, it's here," he insisted. "Look!"

I shrugged. "What's here?"

All I could see was a little piece of metal. It was kind of silver-colored, only dull instead of shiny.

"Right here," he answered. "See?"

I leaned closer. "See what?"

Jake stopped digging. He rolled his eyes when he looked at me.

"A boat!"

I frowned at the tiny piece of metal.

"A boat?"

"Yeah," he answered—his stupid grin stretching from ear to ear, "a boat, an aluminum boat."

I folded my arms and shook my head.

"That's not a boat."

"Is, too," he growled.

"No, it isn't."

He scraped some more sand away. "See?"

I got down on my knees beside him. I still didn't think it was a boat. But, then again, the metal thing he was uncovering did—sort of—look like the front, pointy bow of a canoe.

A little tingle raced up my back. I started digging at the sand on one side. Jake went back to scooping handfuls out on the other. In a matter of seconds, we had enough of the thing uncovered so I could see that it really was a boat!

We dug faster.

After a while, the tips of my fingers felt like they were

on fire. I gently brushed the sand off them, onto my shirt. They were red. They hurt so bad, it wouldn't have surprised me if they started bleeding any second. We only had a small part of the front uncovered, but I couldn't dig anymore. I got up and went after my shovel.

Jake must have felt the same way, because he quit and got up, too. He stretched and rubbed at the sore muscles in his back.

"I bet it's got a motor and everything," he grinned.

I stuck the fingertips of my right hand in my mouth, hoping the spit would cool off the burning.

"Bet it doesn't," I answered. "I bet it's broken in half and this is all there is."

Jake shook his head. "I bet it's all there."

"Then it's got a hole in it or it's all ripped up. *Nobody* throws away a good boat."

Jake bit at his bottom lip.

"Well, maybe it's just got a little hole in it. Maybe we can patch it."

I shrugged. "Maybe so," I said. "One thing's for sure. We'll never know what's wrong with it unless we get it uncovered."

CHAPTER 5

I rubbed at the sore muscles in my back. My shirt was dripping wet, but my only thought when I looked at the long shadows was, Mama's gonna kill me!

Jake made a groaning sound when he got to his feet. It was a lot like the sound Daddy made when he got out of his recliner after watching TV for a long time. Jake stretched and groaned again.

"If it weren't for all these big rocks, we could have had this thing back to your house by now."

I glanced down at the pile of rocks we had removed from the boat and stacked on the bank beside it. Even though we'd removed a ton of them, the boat wasn't even half empty.

Most of the rocks were about as big around as my head. There were some smaller ones and some that were so big it took Jake and me, both, to lift them out of the boat.

Jake wiped the sweat from his forehead with the tail of his T-shirt.

"Why would anybody fill a boat up with rocks?"

I shrugged. "They wouldn't. Not unless they were trying to sink it."

I glanced at the far bank of the river. The lines of long, slender tree shadows had lost their shape and molded into a flat-gray blanket that covered the ground. It was almost dark.

"We've got to get home."

Jake put his hands on his hips and shook his head at the boat. Then he shook his head at me.

"We can't. We've got to get the boat back to your house this evening. If we don't, somebody'll get it."

Sweat had rolled into my right eye. I rubbed it with my thumb, trying to get the stinging to stop.

"Who's gonna get it? Nobody knows it's here."

"Somebody does," Jake answered. "When I found it yesterday, the front point of the bow was sticking out. Today, it was buried. Somebody dug wet sand out of the river and covered it up. If you hadn't had that damp sand stuck all over you, we might never have found it. Somebody tried to hide it. I haven't spent the whole day digging only to have somebody come along and steal our boat tonight."

I nodded my agreement. Jake was right. We *had* worked awfully hard. Mama was going to kill me if I got home after dark. But . . . since I'd missed lunch and dinner . . . well, she was probably going to kill me anyway—so what did it matter?

We got back to work. It was a backbreaking job, tossing the big rocks from the boat and scooping out the loose sand between them with our bare hands. It was dark by the time we got it all emptied out. There was just barely enough light to see.

"Now what?" I asked Jake.

"We take it to your house and put it in the shed."

"How?" I growled. "I'm not dragging that thing up the trail and weaving through all those trees in the dark. If we drag it along the bank, we've got snags and holes and snakes to worry about. As dark as it is, we can't see a thing. Just how are you planning to get it home?"

Jake laced his thumbs into the sleeves of his T-shirt. He pulled the wet material away from his skin, making his chest look twice as big as it really was.

"We'll paddle it home."

I shook my head. "We don't have any paddles. Besides, we don't even know if it'll float."

Jake smiled again. In the dark half-light of early evening, his teeth shone as white as fresh snow.

"We can paddle with our shovels. All we've got to do to see if it floats is shove it into the water. Come on, help me."

He leaned over and started shoving the boat toward the river.

"Shouldn't we dump out the rest of the sand and stuff?"

Jake groaned, then stopped shoving. "We got all the heavy stuff out. We can clean up the rest of it tomorrow."

I bent down beside him. With all our strength, we shoved the boat. It slid over the sand a lot easier than we thought it would. In fact, when it hit the water, Jake had to grab it to keep it from floating off.

We stood for a long time, straining our eyes against the dark. There was no sign of water leaking into the boat. There was still a lot of sand and stuff under the seats and in the back corner, but no water. Finally, Jake motioned to the bank.

"I'll hold the bow here. You go grab the shovels."

I handed one shovel to Jake and kept hold of mine. While he steadied the boat, I climbed in, crawled over the seats, and sat in the back. Jake put one foot in the boat, and with the other, he shoved us into the river.

For a second, I thought we were going to flip over. I quickly leaned one way and then the other. When Jake sat down, the boat leveled.

We spent a few minutes wobbling, rocking, going round and round in circles and bumping into one bank and then the other. After a while, though, we got used to handling our shovel-oars and headed off downstream. The river was low and there wasn't much current. What little there was pushed us easily on our way home.

Even using shovels as paddles, we got home faster on the river than we would have on the path down the bank. By the time we rounded the bend near my house and I could see the light glowing from our back porch, Jake and I had figured out how we were going to keep from being killed.

First off, as soon as we got the boat pulled into the bank, we'd jump out and go racing to the house. We'd both scream and yell and laugh and jump up and down and act so excited that Mama would think we were about to pee in our pants. Then I'd grab the flashlight and Jake would latch onto Mama's arm and we'd drag her out to see the boat. She'd be so impressed by our discovery, she wouldn't even remember she was mad.

CHAPTER 6

I guess Jake and I had a feeling all along that our scheme might not work. I guess that's why, when we pulled the boat onto the shore, we hauled it up the hill and shoved it behind the garden fence before we went tearing off for the house.

We charged into the kitchen, both talking at the same time and laughing and all excited—the way we had discussed. The only trouble was, there was nobody home to hear.

We prowled through the house, trying to figure where everybody was. Finally, Jake found a note pinned to the front screen.

I swallowed the knot in my throat when I read it:

Ben and Jake,

If you come home and find this note
DO NOT LEAVE THE HOUSE.
We are out hunting for you.

The "do not leave the house" part was written in
Magic Marker. It was written real dark and heavy, like
somebody had carved it into the paper instead of writing it.

Jake and I rolled our eyes at each other, then we sat
down on the couch to wait.

I thought the waiting would be the worst part.
It wasn't!

When Jake's and my dad got home, they lectured us
about not letting anybody know where we were and
how worried they were and how they had taken their
flashlights and combed every inch of the bank, downstream from our house.

Then, our dads grounded us—FOR THE REST OF OUR
LIVES!

Mama told us how she and Lisa and Grandma had
searched all over Jacob's Bend, figuring we had gone
there to play and fallen off the cliffs and broken our
necks.

Then she grounded me—FOR TWO WEEKS.

Somehow, the grounding ended up being just three days.

Ordinarily, being grounded for three days wouldn't have been that bad. But with the new boat we'd found just sitting out there in the bushes beside the garden—the three days took *forever*!

Sunday, I slept late, got up, and dressed for Sunday school and church, came home and ate, then sat in my room the rest of the day with a book.

Monday, I read *Big Red*. I'd read it before, but I never got tired of it.

Tuesday morning, Grandma let me help her dig up radishes in the garden. I wasn't that crazy about radishes, but being outside—even for a little while—sure beat sitting in my room.

I was hoping to get to read another book Tuesday afternoon, but *no*, I had to help clean the house. That was lots of *fun*! I had to dust the living room, sweep the bedrooms and the hall, fold the laundry, and make the beds. Then I had to do the dishes.

Jake came over early Wednesday. He had had almost as much fun as I did. Only, instead of one day of doing housework, he got two. We got right to work on our new boat. Grandma gave us a couple of S.O.S. pads from the kitchen, and, before Daddy left to drive his log truck, he lent us an old putty knife from his toolbox.

It took us a long time to scrub all the moss and tarnish off the outside of the boat. When it came to cleaning the inside, Jake came up with a fabulous idea. We went over to his house and got a whole can of Comet. Then we poured it into the bottom of the boat, threw in the two S.O.S pads, and added just enough water to make kind of a soggy paste.

By rocking the boat back and forth, the Comet and pads sloshed around in the bottom, doing the scrubbing for us. We pushed up and down on the boat with our hands for a while. Then we figured it would work just as well if we used the boat like a seesaw. That way our mixture in the bottom of the boat would keep right on cleaning and our arms wouldn't get tired.

Jake sat in the front of the boat and I sat in the back. We were bouncing up and down and having a good old time, when Jake suddenly jumped off.

Just like a seasaw, my end went rushing toward the ground. It jarred me pretty good and I slid off.

"Hey," I yelled, as my seat bounced on the ground.

Jake ignored me. I got up and dusted my jeans off. He was practically standing on his head, searching for something in the bottom of the boat. I scowled at him.

"What's the deal? You could have broken my back, jumping off like that."

"There's something in here," he mumbled. "Rock or something. It keeps rattling around."

"I heard it," I snapped. "That's still no reason to jump off in midair and . . ."

Jake started digging around under one of the seats, trying to pull something out.

"It's an old tackle box," he said. "Look."

He finally got it out from under the seat. It was a metal box with a rusted handle and a latch on it. Jake set it beside the boat and tried to open it. The latch was so caked with rust, it wouldn't budge.

Jake fetched a rock from down the hill. When he came back, he started pounding on the rusted latch. "Hard telling what we'll find in here," he said. "I bet there're all sorts of neat plugs and stuff."

"Yeah," I scoffed, "and I bet every bit of it's rusted or rotted."

Still, the hair at the back of my neck tingled. I stretched up on my tiptoes. My excitement built as I looked over Jake's shoulder while he worked on the latch.

CHAPTER 7

What started out as a tingling at the back of my neck and a little shudder now had me trembling all over. Goose bumps popped out on my arms and back. I rubbed my hand up and down my arm, real fast, trying to make them go away.

Jake and I had taken our "find" to Daddy's garage. It was more the size of a barn than a garage. Daddy had built it so he could drive his log trucks in, out of the rain, when he had to work on them.

I tugged on the string over the workbench that turned the light on. Jake shoved the big, rolling doors shut. When there was just a crack left between the two doors, he stuck his head out. After looking around to make sure nobody had followed us, he finished shutting the doors.

Daddy's workbench was like a big, wooden table, with shelves and cubbyholes, on the far side of the barn against the wall. He worked here on carburetors and other stuff from his truck motors when they broke down. The table was stained with a few oil spots. The smell of gasoline hung heavy in the air.

Jake put the tackle box on the table. Then, looking once again over his shoulder, he opened it and dumped out the contents.

There were about eight fishing plugs. They weren't any good because the hooks were all rusted and matted together. There were two packages of hooks, but the water had seeped into the plastic and they were rusted, too. There was an old spool of fishing line, but it was so old and brittle, it broke with the slightest tug. A bunch of corks filled the rest of the box, but not the little, plastic corks that most people use nowadays. These were real cork corks. They were stained and brown from all the years of water seeping into the tackle box. Other than that, they seemed good as new.

Six of the corks had been stuck together with little sticks to make a doll. There was a small, round cork for the doll's head, a big oblong cork for the body, and smaller, skinnier, oblong corks for arms and legs. I held the doll up for a moment, studying it in the light.

It wasn't much of a doll. Still, it was kind of neat the way it was put together.

There was a pocketknife, too. At least, that's what we thought it was. But it was so rusted, you couldn't see the brand name, much less get the three blades to open.

Jake pushed all this stuff aside.

What really had us excited—what had made us scurry into hiding in the barn like a couple of thieves—was an old mason jar.

It was a real old-timey jar, made of glass and with a seal-top glass lid. There was a metal wire bale that you could push down like a clamp to seal the lid tight.

I knew what the bale was for and how it worked because Grandma used to can green beans in jars like this one.

"It's a treasure map," Jake said, trying to twist the glass top off, "I just know it."

I reached over and shoved his hands out of the way. He'd never get the thing open that way. I got a finger under the metal bale and flipped it up. It made a *tink* sound. Then I took the glass lid off and set it beside the jar.

Jake stretched up on his tiptoes, peering into the jar. He turned it over. Two small matchboxes slid out. They were dry as a bone. Then, with trembling fingers, Jake reached in for the thick brown sheet of paper that circled the inside of the jar.

His eyes popped wide when he got hold of it.

"It *is* real!" he exclaimed. "It's not paper. It's leather or something. It's real!"

Ever so carefully, he pulled the rolled map from the jar. Like the matches, it was dry and unharmed.

I scooted closer, leaning against his shoulder as he started to unfold the map. It looked so old, it should have been brittle. I was afraid it might crack or turn to powder when he tried to open it. Instead, the leather was still soft and pliable.

As Jake unfolded it, I could see lines in red and blue. They were faded and old-looking. There were pictures of trees and rocks and grass that stood out against the brown of the leather. Right in the center of the map was a big, black *X*. It was near the middle of an island on the edge of a small lake. On two sides of the lake the drawing made it look like there were straight, rock cliffs. Around the island, there were wavy lines drawn in blue and brown—like water and dirt flowing together.

The island stuck up from the blue-and-brown waves. It was darker brown—like solid ground—and there were three trees growing from it. Right in the center of the three trees was the *X*.

"What is it?" Jake asked.

I shrugged. "Don't know. Looks like brown-and-blue waves. Not water and not ground . . ."

My eyes opened wide. So did Jake's. We looked at each other and, at the very same instant, gasped:

"Quicksand Swamp!"

CHAPTER 8

My heart almost stopped when Lisa shoved the cork doll under my nose. The fried potatoes I'd just swallowed caught in my throat and I thought I was going to choke.

"May I have it, Ben? May I have the doll?"

Somehow, I managed to get my mouth shut. It had flopped open so wide, I was afraid my chin was almost dragging in my plate. Inside my head, I was screaming: Lisa! You rotten, little stink! You've been spying on Jake and me. You stole that doll from our hiding place. I ought to break your dumb neck. I ought to . . .

But I kept my cool.

Acting real relaxed and like I didn't care, I shrugged.

"I guess. It's just junk, but if you want it . . ."

Mom frowned. She tilted her head to the side, studying the cork doll.

"Lisa, where did you get that?"

Before Lisa could tell her about the knothole in the maple tree that Jake and I used for a hiding place, I broke in. "We found it in the boat. She can have it." I stuffed another spoonful of potatoes into my mouth. "I don't know why she'd want it, though. Thing's stinky and grungy. She's got lots better dolls under her bed that she never plays with. But . . ."

"Don't talk with your mouth full," Grandma scolded.

"Yes, ma'am."

Everybody went back to eating, so it seemed like the conversation was over. I swallowed a piece of bacon and glanced up at Lisa.

My eyes were squeezed so tight, I could barely see. If I could have killed her with my look, I would have. Only Lisa didn't even notice.

What really scared me was that maybe she had the map, too. If she did, I'd choke it out of her if I had to. The map was ours. Jake and I had found it—and whatever treasure was under the big, black X—that was ours, too.

As soon as we finished breakfast, I helped clear the table and took off for Jake's. On the way over, I planned to stop by the maple tree.

"I'm going to Jake's," I called from the front door.

In the kitchen, Mama called back, "Don't forget the church social at the Grissam's tonight."

"I won't."

"Ben?"

"Yes, ma'am."

"Come here."

"But, Mama . . ."

"Ben."

I was in a hurry to get to Jake's and tell him about Lisa finding our hiding place. Still, there was an edge to Mama's voice that made me trot back to the kitchen.

"Yes, ma'am?"

She cocked an eyebrow, looking at me.

"You and Jake have been having a hard time figuring when it's time to come home. Your grandmother is looking forward to the church social. You need to be home at least an hour before dark, so you can get ready. If you're late, like the last time you and Jake took off, well, it will be more than a grounding. Do you understand?"

"Yes, ma'am."

Mama glared at me. "I mean it."

"Yes, ma'am. We won't be late, I promise."

I turned toward the door, and Mama popped me with her dish towel. I jumped and rubbed at my seat, but it really didn't hurt.

"Love you," she smiled. "Be careful."

I smiled back. "We will."

For six years, Jake and I had been using the knothole in the old tree to hide our secret messages and the "neat" stuff we found along the river. The tree was about halfway between our houses and was the best hiding place anybody could ever hope for. Now, this *super* hiding place was gone. Since Lisa had discovered it, we couldn't use it anymore. I couldn't help wondering how long she had known about it.

I guess, when you have a little sister, you just don't have any privacy at all!

When I got to the tree, I leaned my face close to the hole and blew as hard as I could. I waited a second, then blew again.

Jake and I always did that, just in case a spider had crawled inside. The hole was too high off the ground for snakes to reach, but if a spider had made a home inside, blowing would make him climb up to see what was going on.

When nothing popped out, I reached in. I could feel the old, rusty hatchet we had found last year. I could feel the metal Velvet tobacco box Jake and I put our notes in, and I could feel the jar we had found yesterday. Carefully, I pulled it out. The matches and the map were still inside. I heaved a sigh of relief and put the map in my pocket. Then I put the jar back in the knothole.

We'd have to find another hiding place for our secret things. But right now, I needed to find Jake. I took the map with me, just in case Lisa came back.

Jake was curled up on the couch watching early morning cartoons on TV. When I told him about Lisa showing up with the doll at breakfast, he was as mad about her finding our hole as I was.

"We'll never find another hiding place that good," he sighed.

It took Jake less than a minute to get his clothes on. Outside, he took off toward the shed.

"Come on, we've got to get some stuff."

"What?"

"Come on."

Jake had a bad way of never answering me when I asked him something. I followed him to the shed. There, he got his fishing rod and tackle box. Then he went over by his dad's workbench and started touching some wooden boards.

"They're dry," he called, almost laughing. "Here."

With that, a board came flying across the room at me. I blinked and ducked, but still managed to catch it. It was a paddle.

"Dad and I made them while I was grounded," Jake told me. "He carved the shape out of some old two-by-fours he had lying around. I sanded them down, real good, and yesterday we put the last coat of varnish on them."

I looked at the paddle in my hand. It was as good as anything you could buy at Bleue's Hardware Store in town. It was almost as tall as I was, with a handle at the top, a slim neck, and a square blade.

Jake threw the other paddle to me. Then he picked up his fishing gear in one hand and a small plastic bucket in the other.

"What's that for?" I wondered.

"In case the boat leaks," he answered.

I shrugged.

"It didn't leak the other night."

Jake nodded. "That's what I told Dad, but he said that was *before* we cleaned it up. With all that sand and dirt and crud in it, we really couldn't tell. He said we might have to redo the seals on the bottom if they cracked loose."

My forehead wrinkled as my eyebrows shot up.

"Why the fishing rod and tackle box? We're taking the map to see if there's a treasure, right?"

Jake sneered at me.

"Right. So, you want to take an ad out in the paper? Tell everybody we found a treasure map and we're out hunting for gold or jewels or something?"

"Huh?"

Jake shook his head.

"We're taking the fishing stuff 'cause we're going fishing. If we don't, people might get suspicious."

"Like what people?" I scoffed.

"Like anybody." He leaned his face close to mine, looking me straight in the eye. "We're not hunting for a quarter somebody dropped out of their pocket. That map's a real treasure map. Whatever's at the end of it is probably worth . . . well . . . hard telling how much it's worth. We can't take any chances. Somebody could beat us to the treasure. Somebody could be watching for us to find it, then knock us over the head and steal it. We can't let anybody know—not even our parents."

With that, he whirled around and started off toward my house.

All I could do was shake my head. I stood there and watched him. Jake was really nuts, sometimes. I mean, who knew about the map? Besides, there probably wasn't even a treasure.

Still . . .

I took off, trying to catch up with Jake. I felt a little confused inside, a little confused and a little edgy, too.

Treasure hunting had sounded like a fun, silly, harmless way to spend the summer. Now it seemed a little more serious.

Then, again, Jake was probably just trying to be dramatic or something. He was kind of like that—always reading mysteries at school during silent reading time and letting his imagination get away from him.

CHAPTER 9

The boat was a lot easier to handle, now that we had all the rocks and dirt out of it. In fact, it took us a little while to get used to it. It seemed like every time one of us leaned one way or the other, the boat would tip.

It was kind of like learning to balance a bicycle. But in no time at all, we could move our boat around the river without rocking like we were about to flip over.

We spent a while paddling around the back of our house. We'd paddle upstream and let the slow current carry us home again. Grandma came out and worked in her garden for a while, but as soon as she went in the house, we headed downstream toward Quicksand Swamp.

"I've got to be home at least an hour before dark," I told Jake.

He nodded. "Me, too. Daddy said if I make us late for the church social, he'll kill me."

It was about a mile and a half from my house to where Quicksand Swamp started. We paddled for a while, trying to judge the slow current and to figure how long it would take us to paddle back. After a time, we put our paddles down and got out our fishing stuff.

I couldn't help watching the bank. Jake's spooky warning that somebody might be watching as we searched for the treasure made me as nervous as a cat in a room full of rocking chairs. My eyes scanned the bank, like I was expecting to see an Indian in war paint behind every rock, or a gangster with a machine gun behind every tree.

At one point, a tingly feeling crept up the back of my neck—that feeling you get when someone or something's watching you. I made a little snorting sound, trying to laugh it off. Jake's imagination was so big, it even had me going.

It took us nearly an hour to paddle and fish our way downstream. Finally, we rounded a bend in the river, where we could see the banks disappear into flats and where the river spread out among the tall trees.

"Let me see the map," Jake said, after we'd paddled around awhile.

I reached in my pocket and pulled out the map. Before I handed it to him, I glanced at it again. "The channel leading to the lake or pond should be right up ahead," I noted.

Jake studied the map for a minute, then stuffed it into his pocket. "Let's go," he whispered.

As we paddled, we kept a constant watch on the left bank. According to our map, the channel to the pond went between two big, bald cypress trees on our left after we rounded the curve in the main channel.

The only trouble was, there were a lot of *big* bald cypress trees. There were lots and lots of trees and lots and lots of bushes and lots and lots of everything else you would find in a swamp—only, there was no channel.

"Maybe it's around the next bend," Jake said.

"Maybe."

We could tell when we came to the end of Quicksand Swamp. Both sides of the bank rose up and the river narrowed into a channel again, instead of being spread out through the trees. Farther above the river, there were hills and grass and pines.

"We must have missed it," Jake said.

I didn't answer, but I nodded. We turned the boat around and started back. Once more, I got that strange, eerie feeling that someone or something was watching us. I made myself quit thinking about it, though.

"Let me see the map again," I said when we returned to what I remembered as the first bend.

Jake unfolded it and passed it to me.

I studied the blue lines, the tall, bald cypress trees, the curve in the river. "It's got to be someplace, right in here. Why can't we find it?"

Jake kept paddling while I was studying the map. "Things change," he puffed. "I mean, as old as that map must be . . . well . . . trees die. The river could have changed course. The channel could have clogged up with dirt and dead trees and stuff. Who knows?"

He put his paddle down and started fishing. I worked on the map awhile longer, turning it one way, then the other, trying to find something along the swamp that might match. With a sigh, I finally folded it and stuffed it back in my pocket.

Just as I leaned down to get my rod and reel, the boat lurched. The sudden movement almost pitched me from my seat. I stuck a hand out to keep from bumping my head on the bottom of the boat.

"Come on, man," I complained, "quit rocking the . . ."

But as I glanced up, I could see his rod. The thing was almost bent double. Jake's line was stretched tight as a bowstring and it shot back and forth through the water. Jake had a fish. It was a good one, too.

"Hang onto him," I urged. "Don't let him get off."

Jake's jaw was set. His teeth were clamped together so hard I could almost hear them grinding. The boat started to turn a little, following the pull from the other end of the line.

"Watch that brush! Don't let him get tangled in it!" My eyes popped wide open as I saw the line make a run at another pile of brush in front of us. I grabbed the paddle and tried to back us up. "Keep the tip of your rod up," I yelped, my voice so high and excited I sounded like Lisa playing with one of her dolls. "Don't let him break off! Don't let him get hung!"

All Jake could do was grunt and grind his teeth as he fought whatever was on the other end of the line.

It seemed like an eternity before Jake finally got the fish up beside the boat. We'd never caught anything big enough to need a net, but I sure wished we had one now.

"Don't lose him," I gulped.

Jake lifted the tip of his rod and brought the front half of the fish out of the water. The fish was huge. It was a bass. His mouth was big enough for me to stick my whole fist into. Jake lifted him higher.

My hands shook as I gripped my paddle. My knuckles turned white. "Get your thumb in his mouth. Don't let him break off."

Jake reached for him.

"Man, Jake," I gasped, "don't lose him . . . please! Don't lose him. . . ."

CHAPTER 10

The fish flopped around on the bottom of the boat for only a couple of seconds before I leaped over the brace bar and clamped down on him with both hands. As soon as I had him pinned, Jake grabbed a stringer out of his tackle box and ran it through the fish's gill and out its mouth. He tied the other end to the brace bar.

Our boat was flip-flopping and tipping from side to side as the two of us leaped and moved around. We hardly noticed because we were so intent on not letting go of the fish. As soon as we had him tied on the stringer, Jake told me to hand him another stringer from my tackle box. He pulled it through the gills on the other side of the fish's head and tied it to the brace bar behind his seat.

Once we had him tied, we went back to our seats. We were both panting and breathing hard. The fish flopped a couple of more times and then just lay there. I was shaking all over from the excitement. So was Jake.

"Man," he puffed, "I bet he'll go eight pounds."

Jake's smile was so big it stretched his whole face. "That's some fish, isn't it, Ben?"

I nodded so hard I almost broke my neck. "Sure is, Jake. . . ." I could hear my voice tremble. "You played him perfect! There're a hundred snags he could of gotten tangled up in, but you landed him, all right!"

Jake started laughing. We both did. We laughed and giggled and shook our heads—but mainly, we stared down at that fish.

"I bet he's nine pounds," Jake said.

"At least," I agreed.

When you catch a fish, you keep fishing. But when you catch a fish like this one, you don't risk losing it by accidentally flipping the boat over, or having him flop out—you take him right home to show somebody.

We grabbed our paddles and headed upstream. When we got to the riverbank at the back of my house, we pulled our boat clear up on the bank before we started untying the fish. By the time we got him in the house, Jake was saying, "I bet he'll go twelve pounds!"

We put the fish in the sink. His head hung over the edge at one end. His tail hung over the other side. Grandma was excited. She said it was big enough to fillet. Mama said something about what "great" fishermen we were. Lisa only wrinkled up her nose and said, "Oooh, it looks yucky."

Mama had a set of scales that she got for Weight Watchers a couple of years back when she was on this diet. While she hunted for them, Jake and I went out to the barn and got the fish scales out of Daddy's tackle box.

"Six pounds, eight ounces," Mama announced when we came back.

She had to put the scales on top of a Post Toasties box so the fish's head and tail wouldn't be on the counter. With Daddy's scales, there was a hook on the bottom and a handle on the top so you could hold the fish up. Jake hooked the fish's bottom lip and lifted.

At the same time, we both leaned forward to read the scales and clunked our heads together. We laughed, then carefully squeezed in to look at the scales.

Squinting, I held my breath.

Six pounds, four ounces.

It didn't take long to figure Mama's Weight Watcher scales were more accurate.

"He probably dried out some from being in the

bottom of the boat." I sighed. "I bet if we'd weighed him right after we caught him, he would have gone eight pounds."

Jake nodded.

"Six pounds is a beautiful fish," Mama said. "Take him out back, and I'll go get the camera."

She went to the bedroom and got Daddy's Polaroid out of the dresser. She took about three pictures of Jake and his fish, with the river as a background. Then she let me stand beside him and took a couple more.

As soon as she was finished, we ran to the picnic table where she'd laid the photos and waited for them to develop. The color and shapes were already starting to come through on the first picture she'd shot.

Mama came up behind us and put her hands on our shoulders. "They're all coming out real good," she said. "Jake, if you can stay for lunch, I'll clean him."

Jake glanced at her and nodded his head. Then he went right back to watching the pictures.

While Mama was frying the fillets in the skillet, Grandma put a pan of corn bread in the oven and fixed some fried okra. It was the best fish I ever ate. In fact, it was so good even Lisa ate some of it.

As soon as we had finished, Jake wiped his face with his napkin. I heard a little burp.

"Excuse me," he said. "Come on, Ben, let's go see if

there's another one like that down by Quicksand Swamp."

There was a tinkling sound as Grandma dropped her fork. "You boys stay out of Quicksand Swamp," she scolded. "One time, when I was a little girl, this deer hunter by the name of . . ."

Jake and I glanced at each other, and my eyes rolled. Grandma was always telling stories. *This one*, we must have heard at least ten times before. It was about this guy who walked into Quicksand Swamp and never came out. Grandma had other stories, too, but we had heard every one of them. I put my napkin down and started to move back from the table. A quick look from Mama stopped me.

She didn't need to say anything—I knew what her look meant. I'd heard it before: "Your grandmother's getting old," she would say. "She loves to tell you about the old days. The least you can do is put up with it."

When Grandma was finished, we assured her that we would stay in the boat and in the river. We promised that there was no way we would go into the swamp.

But that afternoon Quicksand Swamp is exactly where we went.

CHAPTER 11

When we got back to the bend in the river where Jake had caught his bass, we fished for a while. Treasure hunting was exciting, but so was fishing. Besides, we *knew* there were fish in here. With the treasure . . . Well, we were stuck until we could figure out where the channel was.

The only trouble was, the sun blazed down on us so hard that we felt like a light bulb was sitting on the back of our necks.

We moved closer to the trees, first, because we were hot and needed to get in the shade and second, because Jake's dad told him that fish don't have eyelids like people do. Fish have to stay in the shade because they can't close their eyes. On a bright, sunshiny day, you were more likely to catch them under a dock or a bridge or under a big, shady tree.

The bad thing about moving under the trees was that almost every time we cast our plugs, one of us got our lines caught in the sticks and moss and stuff on the bank. If that happened, all we had to do was reel in our lines and drag ourselves over to shake the plugs off whatever they were stuck on.

The more we fished, the better we got at not getting hung. But, aside from one little-bitty perch that I landed, we didn't catch a thing.

"It's about time to head home," I told Jake, glancing up at the sun.

"Just a couple more casts," he said. "See that pile of logs over there? I bet there's one lying right in front of them. Watch this."

His cast landed short. He made a grumbling sound in his throat and reeled it back fast. I put my rod down in the bottom of the boat and picked up my paddle.

"If we're late for the social, we're really gonna catch it."

"Just one more." With that, Jake threw his plug at the pile of logs again. This time, instead of falling short, the plug whistled through the air and landed with a plop somewhere on the far side.

Jake tried to reel in, but he was stuck. I sighed and put my paddle down. "Come on," I urged, "get loose. We gotta go."

We floated over to the pile of logs, but Jake was hung on the other side. The logs were so high, we couldn't see his plug.

Jake stood up. The boat pitched one way, then the other. I grabbed the sides and held on for dear life. Jake sat down so hard that my end of the boat bounced up like the end of a seesaw.

Finally, when we stopped rocking and bouncing, Jake looked back at me.

"Sorry, Ben, I didn't have my balance."

He steadied himself by reaching for the top log and started to stand again.

"Wait, Jake," I yelped, "don't grab hold of that. That pile of logs looks like a great place for a snake or something."

His hand jerked back as if he'd touched a hot skillet.

"You're right, but that's my favorite plug."

We sat there awhile. Jake scratched his head. Then, at last, he picked up his paddle. He beat on the top log a second, then jabbed the paddle at the pile, like some giant, wooden sword. When nothing came slithering out, he stood up again.

He caught hold of the log for balance, and I steadied the back of the boat. This time, we hardly rocked at all.

"Ben," he called, "you ought to see this. There's a channel up here. It's open water. It winds back into the swamp."

I shook my head.

"Get the plug loose. We've got to go."

"I'll hold the boat. You've got to come see this."

"We don't have time," I growled. "We're gonna be late."

Jake reached down behind the logs to get his plug. I heard kind of a tinkling sound as he tried to pull it free. Even from behind him, I could see the frown that tugged down the corners of his mouth.

"What in the world . . ." he huffed. "Ben, get up here. Come look."

I glanced at the sun. If my guess was right, we only had about an hour to paddle back up the river, get our baths, and get to the church social. If we were late . . . well . . . Mama would kill me for sure.

"We're gonna be late."

"I don't care. Get up here!"

I threw my hands in the air. If Jake was the cause of Mama killing me—somehow, I was going to come back as a ghost or something and spend the rest of my days haunting him.

Carefully, making sure I had my balance, I got up. We tipped a little when I climbed over the seat, but Jake steadied us.

Just like he said, there was an open channel. It was blue water—a little trail that wound its way through the swamp. It was kind of like a small road, only made of water instead of dirt.

"It's a channel," I said. "So?"

Jake glanced around nervously, like somebody might be watching.

"So . . . it's like on the map. Remember? This is it. This is what we've been looking for!"

I jerked. Jake was right. This *was* the channel—the little, blue line on the map that wound its way into Quicksand Swamp.

"And look at this." He pointed down to where his plug was stuck.

I tilted my head to one side, then the other.

"What is it?"

Jake shrugged. "Looks like some kind of fence or something."

I studied it a moment, then reached over the pile of logs and felt it. It was iron or metal, about as big around as my little finger. The metal was formed in rectangles, about eight inches wide and six inches high.

"They're cattle panels," I explained to Jake. "Daddy bought a calf to fatten up last year, so we could have some meat for the winter. He built a little pen out of this stuff."

"What's it doing here?"

I shrugged. "Maybe it washed down during a flood or something and got stuck in this logjam."

"No," Jake said, shaking his head, "look."

I followed where his finger was pointing and found another pile of logs. I had to squint, but I could see another cattle panel behind them. The metal was rusted and dark brown like the logs, but now that I knew what I was looking for, I could make it out.

"And over there." Jake pointed farther.

The more we looked, we discovered that the logs and metal were laid out along the bottom like a fence. It didn't lay in a straight line, but weaved and meandered this way and that. In some places, it was really hard to see because tree limbs covered the logs, or bushes grew up in front of them. Still, we could see the line.

"Why would somebody put up a fence in Quicksand Swamp?" Jake wondered aloud. "I mean, there's no way a cow could live down here. Sheep, either. Why would . . . ?"

"I don't know," I cut him off, "and I don't care." I let go of the log and made my way back to my seat. "What I *do* know is that if we don't get home in time to get ready for that thing tonight, we're dead meat."

"But we found the channel," Jake complained.

"We can come back tomorrow. Now get your plug loose and come on."

"But . . ."

"Jake!"

"But . . ." Jake's mouth curled up on one side, then he pulled his plug loose and flopped down in the boat. We bounced and rocked some, then headed home as fast as we could paddle.

CHAPTER 12

Theodore Grissam had the only green grass in the whole town. That's because he had one of those built-in sprinkler systems that watered his whole lawn early in the morning. Sometimes on the weekend, when Jake and I would go fishing real early, we saw it going. It probably cost Mr. Grissam a lot to run it, but being a banker, I guess he had the money. Besides, that green grass sure was pretty.

If I hadn't had on my good clothes, I would have just plopped down on it and tried to soak up some of that green.

In fact, that was the only bad thing about a church social—you had to wear nice clothes. It wasn't like going to church. I mean, I didn't have to wear my best shirt and pants. Mama did make me put on a clean shirt and my new jeans. That meant I couldn't crawl around on the ground or play anything that might make me fall and get stains on my knees.

We weren't really late, but late enough so Mama and Grandma hurried me up while I was getting dressed.

We walked to the Grissams', since it wasn't that far from our house. Everybody carried a dish. Grandma had fixed a bowl of beans and new potatoes with a mushroom sauce. Mama had fried up a big bowl of chicken, and Lisa had fixed a Jell-O and Cool Whip salad. Daddy had his famous strawberry/banana home-made ice cream. He didn't say anything to me, but I could tell he was a little griped because I hadn't gotten home in time to help him crank the ice-cream maker.

Once we put the stuff on the long tables that lined the Grissams' patio, we all split up and started visiting with folks.

Aside from Lester Volks, who was kind of a pest, and the Badtlow twins, who were downright mean, there wasn't anybody my age there. So I milled around and watched the road for Jake and his dad. When I finally spotted them coming up the long, cement driveway, I walked out to meet them.

"Ben Wilkins," a cheerful voice called, "I'm glad you and your folks could make it."

I looked around and saw Mr. Grissam. Even at an

informal thing like the church social, he had on his gray pin-striped suit and his fancy alligator boots. He was kind of a strange-looking little man—squatty and bent with bowlegs that I could see even under his baggy pants. He stuck out a hand.

We shook and I said, "Thank you for having us at your home." (It was what Mama taught me to say—even when I was someplace I didn't want to be.)

He shook my hand a little harder and longer than I thought he should. Then he let go and put a hand on my shoulder.

"I've been meaning to contact you," he said softly. "I wanted to apologize."

I frowned.

"What for?"

"The other day, when you came into the bank. Well . . . I . . . er . . ." He stammered a moment, then cleared his throat. "Well, it was four years after my son disappeared. I was thinking about him instead of really listening to you . . . and . . ."

"That's all right, Mr. Grissam," I interrupted, "I understand."

". . . and I wanted to let you know I am sorry," he went on. "It's not right to ignore somebody who comes into the bank." He smiled. "Now then, you said something about needing a loan?"

I looked down at the ground. Talking to grown-ups

always made me a little nervous. I scraped the toe of my shoe back and forth on the concrete. Just a couple of inches from my foot, I could see Theodore Grissam's alligator boots. I couldn't help thinking to myself how fancy and nice they looked. Someday, if I had the money, I'd like my daddy to have a pair just like them.

When I looked up, Mr. Grissam was smiling at me. I felt a little strange when he did that. As long as I could remember, he always had a serious, sad look on his face. I couldn't ever remember him smiling. But I smiled back anyway.

"Jake and I were gonna fix up a couple of lawn mowers so we could earn some money this summer. But since it hasn't rained in a coon's age, there's no grass. It was a dumb idea."

Mr. Grissam ruffled my hair. (I hated it when grown-ups ruffled my hair.)

"It'll rain," he chuckled, "sooner or later. It always does. When it does, let me know if you and Jake still need that loan. I'm sure we can work something out."

He fluffed my hair again, then went back toward the tables to greet the Johnsons who had just arrived. I smoothed my hair down and went to get Jake.

Kenny Grissam, Mr. Grissam's brother, reached him before I did. He had on his jeans and a bright-colored cowboy shirt. (He looked a lot more relaxed than his brother.) He whispered something to Jake's dad, then shook hands with Jake. I was too far away to hear what they were talking about, but Jake nodded a couple of times, then his face got kind of red and he laughed. Jake's dad went off with Kenny, and Jake came to meet me.

"What was that all about?" I asked.

Jake's cheeks turned a little pink. "I like that Kenny Grissam," he grinned. "He's crazy."

I cocked my eyebrows, waiting.

"He said that his brother told him about us wanting a loan so we could get a new boat. He said if we'd come to him, he would have been glad to help us out. Said he wasn't a tightfisted snob like his brother Theodore. Then he told Dad that he and some of the other guys were going out to his truck because he just came across a jug of fresh moonshine. He said it wouldn't be long before I could join them, because I was almost grown up enough." Jake swallowed. "That kind of embarrassed me, with Dad standing there."

He blinked a couple of times. "Come on, let's go see what's going on. We're too young to have anything to drink, but I bet they'd let us stand around and listen. I bet your dad'll be there, too."

I shook my head. My mouth kind of twisted up at one side.

Kenny Grissam always had a jug of fresh moonshine in his truck. Always! I remembered, a few years ago, I'd been standing around when he came up and asked Daddy if he wanted to join the guys around back. Daddy was real polite when he said "No, thanks," and when Kenny left, he told me that he wasn't opposed to a "snort" every now and then, but he just didn't think a church social was the right place for it.

I knew Daddy wouldn't be there. And besides, standing around a bunch of old men drinking booze wasn't my idea of a "fun time." The fact was, I didn't even like it when they came back from Kenny's truck and said "Hi" to me. The smell of their breath, after they'd had some of that stuff, was enough to make me barf.

Anyway, I shook my head again. "Nah. Let's go see what Tiffany and Lisa are doing. I think they're out in the playhouse."

"You don't want to see what Tiffany and Lisa are doing," Jake said, poking me in the ribs with his elbow, "you just want to see if Sandy's there."

"Do not!" I snarled.

"Do too!"

"Do not!"

Jake laughed. "You're gonna see if she's out there so you can play house." He giggled. "Or maybe play kissie-face."

I slugged him on the shoulder. I hit Jake harder than I had intended to. My knuckles popped and my wrist turned. Jake kind of stumbled and grabbed his shoulder. My hand hurt.

"Hey," he yelped.

"I don't even like Sandy," I lied. "She's a geek."

Jake's eyes almost twinkled. "You'd still like to play kissie-face with her," he teased. "I bet that if you ever got her alone . . ."

I doubled my sore fist and swung at him again. Every time I tried to get close enough to punch him, he'd dance out of my reach. He moved backward, ahead of me, toward Tiffany's playhouse.

Finally, I just ignored him. Once I did that, he quit teasing me.

Tiffany's playhouse was like the Grissams' house, only smaller. It had big pillars in front and a steep pointed roof. It was painted white with green trim around the door and the little windows. Inside, there was a twin bed, a couple of rocking chairs, and plenty of room for Tiffany's dolls, her toy refrigerator and range, and all that stuff.

Tiffany and Lisa were the only ones there. In a way, I was glad Sandy wasn't around. Jake would just say something to embarrass me. In another way . . . well, Sandy *was* cute. She had long, smooth hair and eyes that sparkled. When she'd smile at me, it made me feel a little funny inside.

Lisa and Tiffany were both sitting on the twin bed.

Tiffany was playing with a big doll that had a china face and hands. It had a long, frilly dress with expensive-looking lace all over it. It probably cost more than two new fishing rods and reels and a whole box of plugs to go with them. Lisa—well, she had a little rag doll that Grandma had made for her.

But for some strange reason, Lisa seemed to be having just as much fun playing with her little, junk doll as Tiffany was playing with her expensive one.

They looked up and said "Hi." I waved back and shut the door.

There was a wood bench about twenty yards behind the playhouse. I motioned Jake over to it, and we sat down to start making plans for tomorrow.

About then, the grown-ups called that it was time to eat. Reverend Barker said a prayer (it seemed to last forever), and after everybody ate and visited for a while, we headed home.

It wasn't until we got inside the house that Mama and Grandma noticed the doll.

"Where on earth did you get that?" Mama asked.

I put the pan I carried home on the kitchen table and glanced over at Lisa. She was clutching Tiffany's big china doll.

"Tiffany gave it to me," she answered. "We traded."

"You traded?" Grandma said, coming over beside her for a closer look. "What did you trade?"

Lisa smiled happily.

"The little rag doll you gave me."

Mama's mouth fell open. Grandma almost dropped the casserole bowl. And at the same instant, they both yelped, "That rag doll???"

Lisa shrugged. "Yeah. Tiffany said it was pretty, so we traded."

Mama and Grandma looked at each other and shook their heads. Mama put her pan in the sink and came over to Lisa. She sat in one of the kitchen chairs and pulled Lisa onto her lap.

"You can't keep it," she explained gently. "That doll Tiffany gave you is very, very expensive. It's a china doll and there's even lace on the dress. That doll you gave her was made out of rags. It didn't even have a dress."

"But, Mama, Tiffany was the one who wanted to trade."

Grandma shook her head. "It's not right."

Mama nodded in agreement. "It isn't right, Lisa. You know how we've taught you to be fair. Well a trade like that just isn't fair."

Lisa's bottom lip stuck out.

"But tomorrow I was going to take the cork doll that Ben gave me. Tiffany said she really wanted to see *it*, and that maybe we could trade again."

Mama smiled.

"I'm sorry, baby. First thing in the morning we'll

have to take this one back. You can show Tiffany the cork doll. But no more trading. You *do* understand, don't you?"

Lisa's bottom lip started to quiver. Then, real quick, she sucked it back in her mouth and kind of bit on it. "I understand," she said, nodding. "May I stay and play with her some, when we take it back?"

Mama hugged her tight. "You may stay and play."

I had a hard time getting to sleep that night. I guess part of it was the excitement about going treasure hunting tomorrow.

Most of my problem getting to sleep, though, was Lisa.

As long as I could remember, Jake and I had wanted a boat. A real boat. One with a motor and seats. One that was big enough and fast enough to take out on Broken Bow Lake. There were islands and channels and all sorts of great places to fish. We would take our dads. And when we were in school, our dads could use it to take people out. They could be fishing guides and earn money doing something they liked.

Without ever saying anything to each other, Jake and I both knew that if the map *really* did lead us to a treasure, a boat was the first thing we'd buy.

There probably wasn't a treasure, though. It was probably just a silly dream.

But if there was—the first thing I was going to do, even before buying the boat, was get Lisa a nice, pretty doll that she could play with as much as she wanted. A doll even nicer and prettier than any Tiffany had.

I was going to get Lisa a doll she could be proud of.

CHAPTER 13

Since we'd already found the channel, it took us hardly any time to locate it again. Jake had brought along a stick so he could beat on the logs to make sure there weren't any snakes around. That way, he wouldn't dent the paddle that he and his dad had made.

When Jake was sure there were no snakes, he climbed up on the logs and held the front of the boat.

"Come on," he motioned, "we'll drag the boat over."

It took a lot of tugging and straining and wrestling to get the boat up on the logs. Being aluminum, it was light, but it still made for sweat-popping work because of the logjam being high and because of the junk we had in the boat. We were careful not to get water in the front end when we slid it down the other side of the logs.

The channel twisted and wound its way through the swamp. We followed it for probably a quarter of a mile or more, then there was another log pile.

Like the first one we found, the logs were laced to a metal fence. It seemed higher than the first jam and it took us longer to get the boat over it. When we had our boat in the water on the other side, Jake climbed to his seat. I got in the rear and pushed us off.

The water in this part of the channel seemed a lot clearer than in the first part. It was a bright blue, and I could see old logs and stumps beneath the surface. A couple of times I saw small turtles swim under us as we passed.

The swamp on either side of the channel smelled of damp and rotted wood. There were a few trees, but most were dead. They had no limbs, but were just tall stumps, reaching like bare poles toward the sky. It isn't good for trees to stand in water all the time. The farther we got, the more dead trees we saw, until there was almost as much brown as green in the swamp beside us.

We saw a couple of squirrels playing in a big cypress tree. Now and then a frog went *plop* in the water when we rowed toward him, and turtles slipped off logs. But mostly it was quiet. The damp swamp air hung heavy all around us.

We rounded a little bend in the channel, and suddenly the swamp disappeared. A wide, smooth, clear, blue pond stretched out before us. And there, not more than two hundred yards across the pond, was an island—the island where the treasure of Quicksand Swamp was buried.

It was one of the prettiest little ponds I ever saw. It was about twice as big as our high-school football field. To the left, a ridge of rock stuck up about six feet, straight out of the water. Beyond the little ridge, I could see the swampy bottom stretching out for at least half a mile. There was another little ridge of rock on the right, making the pond look like it was set in a small bowl carved out by nature.

Except for some logs that floated near the banks on each side, the surface of the water was as smooth and shiny as the bottom of Grandma's old cast-iron skillet. As we moved from the channel into the pond, I could see sunken trees beneath us. Their branches stretched toward the surface like ghostly fingers reaching for the sky.

Our boat cut through the glassy-smooth water like a hot knife slipping through a pat of butter. There was no wind, and the only sound we heard was the little slap of water against the sides of our boat as we paddled toward the island.

I guess we were more excited about hunting for treasure than I thought. By the time we reached the island, we were paddling so hard and fast, our boat slid halfway up on the bank before we stopped.

We hadn't even skidded to a complete stop when Jake leaped out. He grabbed the shovel closest to him and charged up the bank.

There was a little rise in front of us. It was a mound of dirt with dead logs and sticks piled at the top. He scampered up the little hill and disappeared behind it.

Being stuck in the back of the boat, I took a little longer to get out. Since we stopped kind of uphill, I had to grab the rail and pull myself out. The boat rocked some, since the back end was still in the water. I kept my balance and climbed onto the dry sand. From over the hill, I could hear Jake yelling at me to bring the map.

I pulled the boat a little farther up on the bank. After Lisa had found our hiding place, we'd put the map back in the mason jar in the tackle box we'd found. With the boat well up on the bank, I could reach in and get my tackle box without having to crawl back into the boat. I got my fishing rod and the other shovel, too, then climbed the bank to join my friend. I figured we'd go back to the boat later to get the lunch we'd packed.

"There aren't any trees," Jake's voice squeaked from the far side of the hill. "Hurry up with the map. There aren't any trees."

The whole island wasn't much bigger around than

our gym at school. There was only one tree—kind of off
to the side. The rest of the island was flat and covered
with sand and dirt and dead logs and stuff. A few scrub
bushes added a little green to the place, but other than
that and the tree, there wasn't much to look at.

A little rise, like the one I was standing on, made up
three sides of the island. At the back of the island, there
was a small channel of water, about ten yards wide.
Beyond it, Quicksand Swamp stretched out as far as I
could see.

Jake was walking around in a big circle in the center
of the island. He looked at the tree, then walked a few
feet away, then circled back.

When Jake saw me come over the little hill, he stuck
his shovel in the ground and trotted over. "There's just
one tree," he complained. "It showed three on the
map, didn't it?"

I nodded. "Think so. Let's see."

I knelt down and opened the box. When I tried to get
the map out of the jar, the matches slid out. I shoved
them back in and got hold of the map. Beside me, I
could almost hear Jake panting as I unrolled it.

Sure enough, there were three trees. They made a
triangle, with the big, black X right in the middle.

Frowning, Jake scratched his chin. "We've got to find
those other two trees."

I frowned back. "How do we know how many paces to take from each one?"

Jake shrugged. "It doesn't matter. The X is right in the middle. If we can find where the trees were, we can figure out where to dig. But—we've got to find the trees first. They probably died and fell over or something. Let's go."

It didn't take long to find where the second tree had been. It was an old, jagged stump that was half-buried by dead brush. We must have spent over an hour looking for the third tree, though.

I was about ready to give up when I heard Jake call, "Ben, come look at this."

I went to where Jake was standing. He pointed to a log with his shovel. It was over on its side, and from one end, it had five limbs that stuck out like the points of a star. There was a low spot in the ground—kind of a little, sunken hole, where it had pulled the dirt out when it fell over.

I patted him on the shoulder.

"You found it, all right," I smiled. "This is it, it's the third tree."

Jake got a long pointed stick and jabbed it in the ground, right in the middle of the low spot. Then we went back to the middle of the island. We kept scooting around until we figured we were right in the middle of where the three trees had once stood. When we figured we were "centered," Jake took his shovel and pushed down on the point. He started dragging it to make a big circle.

"It's got to be right in here," he said when he finished drawing the circle. "Someplace right in here!"

I grabbed my shovel and we went straight to the middle of the circle. Dirt flew in every direction. We dug and dug. We were so excited, we even hit each other with shovelfuls of dirt a couple of times.

We had a hole about six feet around and were down as deep as our knees before we stopped. Both of us were puffing and panting and out of breath. I tried to wipe the sweat from my eyes with my hand, but my hand was just about as wet as the rest of me. My eyes stung and I needed a break, so I put my shovel down and took my shirt off. I used it like a towel to wipe the sweat off my head and face.

"I'm getting somethin' to eat," Jake announced. "You want somethin'?"

I glanced back at him over my shoulder. "I'm not hungry yet. Bring the jug of water—I'm dyin' of thirst."

I wiped my face again, then fluffed my hair and hung my shirt over a pile of brush to dry. It felt good to get the sweat off. I took a deep breath and leaned on the handle of my shovel.

"Ben! *Ben*!!"

I jumped.

Jake's voice wasn't a yell—it was more like a scream. Chills raced up my back and grabbed at that spot between my shoulder blades. I looked around.

He was standing on top of the knoll, looking down at our boat. He took a couple of steps and disappeared over the little ridge.

"Ben! Come quick," his high-pitched voice shrieked again.

I raced to him. I was running so hard I stumbled going up the ridge. Clambering on all fours, I clawed my way to the top.

Jake stood shivering like somebody in a cold, chilly wind. I tilted my head to the side, wondering why he was acting like that. Then I *saw* why. My hands jerked. My knees almost buckled beneath me.

Our boat was gone!

CHAPTER 14

Jake turned and glared up at me. He had the nastiest, angriest look on his face I'd ever seen.

"It's your fault," he snarled. "You were the last one out of the boat. You were supposed to pull it up on the bank."

"I . . . I . . ." My mouth opened, but "I . . . I . . ." was all I could get out. I started down to where he was, only my feet were frozen.

My jaws clamped together so tight I could hear my teeth grinding inside my head. I glared back at him.

"It wasn't my fault," I finally managed.

"Was, too!"

I was so mad, my feet finally started moving. I stomped down the hill toward him.

"Was not! I pulled it up on the bank. I swear I did!"
Jake just glared at me again.

"Then how'd it drift off?" He pointed across the water. Our boat was nestled against some swamp grass near the little channel where we had come into the pond. "If you pulled it up on the bank," he snapped, "then how'd it get over there?"

My fist doubled up at my side when I got to him. I *knew* I'd pulled our boat up on the bank, but Jake was calling me a liar. I didn't like that. I wanted to punch him so much it hurt. It hurt even more when I didn't.

"I'll show you," I growled. "I'll prove it was up on the bank. I'll . . ."

I looked down the bank where my tackle box and fishing rod were lying. Mumbling to myself, I stomped over to it. Sure enough, there in the sand was the rut where our boat had been. I waved for him to come and look.

Jake studied the rut in the sand. I pointed an angry finger at the place where the boat had been. Then I shook my finger right under Jake's nose.

"See," I snapped, "I told you. Look how far up on the bank it was."

"Yeah," he huffed, "but it was on a steep part of the bank. It must have slipped back into the water. It's your fault."

I looked at the bank. It *was* steep, but not that steep. Besides, I *knew* the boat was solid when I got out of it. There was no way . . .

I looked at my "friend." He just gave me another one of his disgusted glares and sat down on the bank. I felt my eyes roll in a big circle inside my head. There was no sense arguing with him, so I plopped beside him. I landed so hard that I bounced. My teeth rattled in my head. Still furious with him, I started yanking the laces of my tennis shoes.

"All right," I sneered, "so, it's ALL MY FAULT!" (It really wasn't, but that's what Jake wanted to hear—so I'd just show him.) "It's my fault that the boat drifted away. So I'll just go get the darned thing."

Jake didn't say anything. He only sat there and watched me untie my shoes. I yanked my socks off and flung them down. Then I left my pants lumped up on top of my tennis shoes. I stomped into the pond, so hard the water flew in all directions. I smiled to myself, hoping Jake would get wet from the splash. It'd serve him right.

When I got about waist-deep, I squatted down and shoved off from the bottom. The water felt GREAT! It was cooler than the heavy, thick air that hung about Quicksand Swamp. I splashed around a moment, getting used to the feel of it, then I started swimming.

After the sweat I'd worked up digging for that dumb

treasure, swimming felt wonderful. I swam slowly, enjoying the feel of it.

I hadn't gone very far when I heard Jake call from the bank behind me. His voice was kind of like a question:

"Ben?"

I ignored him.

He called my name again. This time his voice was more urgent:

"Ben??!"

As I swam, I glanced back at him over my shoulder. He was looking at something off to the side. His mouth hung open—wide enough for a bald eagle to fly in and out. I rolled over and kept swimming.

The third time Jake's voice came to my ears, it wasn't a question. It was a scream.

"Ben! *Ben!!!*"

Even with water sloshing in my ears, I could hear the panic in his voice. I stopped and treaded water as I turned to look at him.

Jake was like a crazy man. He was jumping around on the bank, leaping from one foot to the other. He pointed at something, jabbing his finger again and again at the water by the left bank of the pond.

"Swim, Ben!" he shrieked. "Hurry. Swim! Ben! *Ben!!!*"

Some water had got in my mouth. I sprayed it out in a little stream.

"What is it?" I called back to him. "What?"

He kept jumping in the air, pointing his trembling finger. "There. In the water. It's coming after you! Swim, Ben! *Swim!!!*"

From down in the water, I couldn't see anything but a big log floating around. But I knew what it was. From up there on the bank, where he could see, Jake had spotted a snake. It was probably slithering around that log. It might even be a water moccasin.

In my mind's eye, I could almost see it wiggling in an S shape as it moved from beside the log toward me.

I started back toward the bank. I wasn't as scared of snakes as Jake was. Daddy had once told me that snakes don't usually bother swimmers. He said that the splash scares them away. About the only way you'd get bitten would be if you stepped on one or swam over the top of one and hit him with your arm or something.

But just to be on the safe side, I'd head back to the bank and get out until the thing swam off.

Jake was still in a panic. He'd stopped jumping around from one foot to the next. Now he was picking up sticks and little logs from the bank. Hard as he could, he was throwing them at the big log.

Dumb move, I thought. The poor snake was probably trying to crawl up out of the water to get dry. If Jake kept chunking sticks at him, he'd have to stay in the water where I was.

"Hurry Ben!" Jake shrieked again. "Swim! He's after you!"

I raised my head and treaded water.

The log was closer now, but for the life of me, I couldn't see a thing swimming around it.

Suddenly, my eyes flashed. Every muscle in my body snapped tight like a steel trap.

"*Swim, Ben! Swim!!*" Jake screamed again.

The log was closer now.

Only it wasn't a log!

It wasn't covered with bark. It was covered with thick, big, warty-looking scales. There were two yellow-green eyes. Two round nostrils. And at the very front of the log, there were teeth—white, shining fangs like those that had snapped at my face when I looked under the tarp in Daddy's truck.

Alligator!!!

The word screamed inside my head. And at that very second, I heard myself screaming, just like Jake was screaming:

"*Swim, Ben! Swim!!!*"

CHAPTER 15

I remember swimming harder than ever before. I remember my arms digging through the water, pulling me forward as fast as they could. I remember my feet fluttering as quick as I could make them. I remember glancing up once, when I took a breath, and seeing that "log" with the scaly, warty snout and white fangs coming closer and closer and closer.

I *don't* remember how I got out on the bank and ran clear up onto the hill with Jake.

Panic? Fear? I don't know what, but something inside just took over and made me swim for my life. I didn't think about it. I don't even guess I knew what I was doing. But somehow, I did it.

I could feel my heart pounding in my ears. I gasped

for breath. I had my arms wrapped around Jake and he was hanging onto me, too. We stood there, on top of that hill, trembling, shaking, gasping for breath, and looking down at the huge alligator.

He glided up to the bank, as smooth and easy as a sailboat pushed by a gentle breeze. I could see all of him now for the first time.

He was a good ten, maybe twelve, feet long. It was like he didn't see Jake and me up on the hill. He sniffed around on the bank, where I had clawed my way out of the water. His wrinkled, warty nostrils didn't move, but he turned his head to the side and shoved it into the sand where my footprints led from the water.

Jake and I still held onto each other for dear life. With one gentle sweep of his enormous tail, the alligator glided a little farther up on the bank. He sniffed at the second track my feet had dug in the sand.

Despite the hot, muggy air of the swamp, a chill shot up my back. It made me shake as hard as on a cold winter evening when I had to gather wood. The alligator was still after me. He was following my tracks.

I wanted to run.

The big alligator raised his body. His short, stubby legs pushed his front end the rest of the way out of the water and he took a couple of slow, hard, laboring steps up the bank.

I had to get away. "*Run*," a voice inside me screamed.

I let go of Jake and started toward the tree—the one near where we had dug for treasure.

Jake had a different idea.

I'd only gotten a step or two when I heard him yelling.

"Get out of here, you stinking . . ." he screamed. "Go on. Get!"

I looked around. Jake was picking up sticks and logs from the top of the hill. Hard as he could, he was throwing them at the alligator.

"I'll bash your darn head in. I'll . . . I'll . . ."

He picked up a log. It was so big, he had to use both hands to throw it. There was a loud, clunking sound as the log landed square in the middle of the alligator's back. The gator's eyes rolled up in his head. His thick, scaly eyelids closed over them. But it was more like a blink, because in an instant, his eyes were open again and he was looking around in the sand to see where I had gone.

Jake picked up another stick. I reached a trembling hand for his arm.

"Don't, Jake, he's gonna come after us. You're gonna make him mad."

Jake threw the stick. It made a white spray as it splashed the water just beyond the huge, scaly monster. He grabbed another stick.

"Come on. Run. He'll get us!" I tugged Jake toward the tree.

Jake yanked his arm from my grip. He threw the stick. This one landed short. It sprayed a little sand against the alligator's side. He didn't even blink.

"The tree." I tugged at Jake's arm again. "Climb the tree. He can't get us up there. Come on."

Jake pulled away from me and reached down for another stick. "He can't get us here," Jake snapped. "They're fast in the water, but slow on land. He won't chase us. Not up here."

He threw another stick. And another and another.

I knew he was wrong. I knew that any second, the alligator was going to charge up the bank after me, fast as a greyhound chasing a rabbit. I braced my left foot in the sand, testing it with my weight to make sure I had good footing and could shove off and run for my life. Then I reached down, got a stick from the ground, and threw it.

As fast and hard as we could, Jake and I threw more sticks at the alligator. Big sticks, little ones—it didn't matter. Whatever we could grab, we threw.

Jake hit him right on the tip of the snout with a pretty good-sized limb. The gator's eyes closed. His short, stubby legs gave way and he plopped on his belly in the sand. Jake moved a bit farther down the bank.

Tree limbs filled the air, coming down like a hail-storm around the alligator. He only lay there.

Then, a small stick that I threw landed right on the big knot where one of his eyes stuck up. Faster than a blink, he lashed his head and tail to the side. He flashed his fangs and snapped his jaws.

With a shudder, I froze in my tracks. When he snapped his jaws, the sound echoed across the pond like the loud crack of a gunshot. The alligator gave one good shove back toward the pond with his front feet. Then he stopped.

Jake started walking around a few feet from me, looking down at the ground. He tilted his head from side to side like he was searching for something. Then he smiled.

Jake had found a limb about ten feet long that was all in one piece. The big end was buried in the sand, but finally Jake wrestled it out.

Then, grunting and straining, he lifted it above his head like some giant club before starting down the bank.

"Be careful," I called. "Watch it. Don't get too close."

The long branch waved and wiggled in the air above Jake's head. He strained and struggled, trying to bal-ance it. When he felt he was in range, he lifted the long log as high as he could. It was so long that he couldn't bring it down like a club. All he could do was balance the thing and let the other end fall.

It was a perfect shot. The heavy end of the log came crashing down, right on top of the big gator's head.

He'd had enough. With one hard push of his short legs and a twist of his powerful tail, the alligator slipped back into the water.

Jake stood there, puffing and rubbing his arm. I held a stick above my head, ready to throw it. Dead limbs and sticks floated and bobbed in the water. We had thrown so many at the gator, we'd almost covered this little part of the pond.

Still holding the stick, I squinted, studying the clutter of sticks and expecting to see the alligator bob up, any second, someplace in the floating mess.

Jake had the same idea. He picked up a stick from the ground, ready to throw it at the first sign of the gator. The minute his head bobbed up, we were going to plaster him again.

We waited.

At last I saw him. With my free hand, I pointed. "There he is. . . ."

At that very same instant, Jake pointed and screamed: "There he is. . . ."

I looked at Jake and Jake looked at me.

My mouth gaped open. The stick I was holding, ready to throw, slipped from my hand. My eyes almost popped out of my head.

We were pointing in opposite directions.

I heard a gulping sound in my throat when I swallowed.

There was more than one alligator!

CHAPTER 16

"Get your foot off my finger," Jake winced.

I moved my foot.

"And quit wiggling around," he said. "You keep knocking tree bark in my hair."

I looked down. Jake glared up at me. The only part of him I could see was his face between my bare feet.

The small branch I clung to was up high in the tree. Jake stood on the bottom branch, but he was holding onto the one where I stood. If it hadn't been for the branch between us, I would have been standing square on top of his head.

Finally, he looked back toward the pond. "I counted eight," he said. "That what you got?"

I shook my head. "No, nine. The big one that came

after me hasn't come back up yet. Either that, or he's on the other side of the boat where we can't see him."

My grip tightened on the branch, but I tried not to move my feet.

The logs we had seen when we first got to the pond weren't logs at all. They were alligators. We had counted at least eight or nine of them from our perch in the only big tree on the island. The one that had chased me was the biggest. The others ranged in size from about four or five feet to eight feet.

Mostly, they stayed near the rock ridges that formed the banks of the pond. But with all the stick throwing and yelling we had done at the big gator, we must have stirred them up. They cruised around. From up here in the tree, we could see their short, stubby legs dangling down and their tails swooshing gently as they swam. They'd glide for a moment, then lay completely motionless with nothing but their eyes and noses above the water.

My toes wiggled a little as I tried to grip the branch with my feet. I tried not to move, though, so Jake wouldn't yell at me. "There he is," I whispered. "He came up by that little short one on the left."

"He *is* huge," Jake whispered back. "He's a monster!"

I don't know how long we stayed in the tree. We kept

watching them. It was almost like I was frozen. In a way, they were beautiful to watch—it was so easy for them to slide through the water and float with only their eyes and nose above the surface. In another way, they were the most ugly, terrifying things I could imagine. They were like something primitive from thousands of years ago; they were like the dinosaurs. My insides felt cold and helpless.

More than anything else, I wanted to be home. I wanted to be with Mama and Grandma and Daddy and Lisa. I wanted to feel safe.

In my mind's eye, I could almost see my family. They wouldn't even be worried about us—not yet. They were probably sitting in the living room, watching TV, or maybe fixing supper or working in the garden. Or maybe . . .

Jake touched my foot. I jumped so hard, I almost fell out of the tree.

I looked down. He was raking the tree bark out of his hair. "We can't stay up here," he said.

I bit at my bottom lip. "I'm sorry. You startled me. I'll be still."

"It's not that," he said, looking up at me. "We've got to do somethin'. We can't stay up in the tree. We'll starve. We've got to find a way to get out of here."

He sat down on the branch where he had been standing. Then, wrapping his arms around it, he slipped off and swung to the ground.

"Wait, Jake."

He kept walking. "Did you get your rod and reel out of the boat?"

I moved down to the branch where he had been.

"Yeah," I called after him, "it's there by my tackle box." Then glancing nervously at the pond, I called, "You better get back up here."

Jake ignored me. He marched right to where the big alligator had chased me out on the bank. There, he plopped on his bottom and opened the tackle box.

When I climbed down out of the tree, I couldn't see Jake because of the little hill that curved around the edge of our island. I trotted to the top of it. That way, I could keep an eye on the pond and the alligators, and at the same time, see what my friend was up to.

He dug around in my tackle box for a while. Then he picked up a plug. Even from behind him, I could see him smile.

"Hello, Little George," he laughed.

I just shook my head as he tied the plug onto the end of my fishing line. Here we were, trapped on an island in the middle of a pond full of alligators—and *he* was going fishing. I wanted to march down there and bop him on the head.

"You dummy," I growled, "do you know how much trouble we're in? Do you know . . ."

He cast the plug. It sailed across the pond, the line floating in a silky arch behind it like the clear, glistening web of a spider. When the plug hit, it made a little splash about twelve feet in front of the boat. Jake reeled in the line and cast again. This time it hit closer, but off to the side.

He was fishing, all right, but he wasn't fishing for fish. He was fishing for our boat.

"Little George" was a small fishing plug. It was small, but it was the heaviest plug in my tackle box. It was called a bottom bumper, because as soon as you cast the thing, it was so heavy that it went straight to the bottom.

With each cast, Jake threw Little George closer to the boat. All he had to do was land one shot, right in the thing. Then, the two sets of three-way hooks would catch on the seat or the metal rim around the stern and he could reel in the boat.

I started toward him. My eyes were darting and jumping around like two ants scampering on top of a hot skillet. I watched Jake, watched the alligators, watched the boat. And somehow, with all that looking and watching, I managed to find my pants, my socks, and my tennis shoes. Never taking my eyes off anything that was going on, I got dressed.

"You gotta throw it harder," I encouraged from right

next to Jake's elbow. "Throw harder. You're landing short."

Jake reeled in and threw again. "I don't want to throw over the boat. If I get it tangled in that brush and lose it, there isn't anything heavy enough in your tackle box to throw that far again."

I watched him make another cast. It was way off. Then, glancing around to check on the alligators, I picked up my tackle box and started looking through it. Jake was right. There were more plugs in there, but most were lightweight. There was a Hola-Popper and a couple of Lucky-13s and about six Abbu-spinners, but nothing near as heavy as the Little George. Then I dug down in one side and found some lead weights and some three-way hooks that I used for catfish. If we lost Little George, I could always rig something up with that.

I started to tell Jake to go ahead and throw. If we lost the plug, we were still safe and could rig up something else. But just as I put the box down and opened my mouth to speak, I heard a loud *clunk*.

The plug had hit the back of the boat. There was a little ripple in the water where it had bounced off. Jake almost had it.

One of the alligators had cruised closer to the boat. Another was moving toward us. I threw a stick in his direction and he stopped.

Jake cast again and again. A couple of times he caught

a stick that we'd thrown at the big gator who chased me. He'd reel it in and unhook the plug, then cast again.

I could hardly stand it. After all, it *was* my rod and reel. I was used to it. I could drop a plug right next to a stump or a lily pad. I mean . . . anybody could do better than Jake. I moved over to take the thing away from him and do it myself.

Then it happened. Little George plopped right in the backseat of the boat.

"Got it," Jake yelped.

"Careful," I coached. "Don't yank it. Don't reel in too fast. You don't want to break the line."

He nodded.

"Slow and easy, Jake. Reel it in careful."

He kept the tip of the rod down. Ever so slowly, he started reeling in. The slack went from the monofilament line. My eyes got wide when the line went tight. I could feel a little tingle run up my back. The boat started to move. Chill bumps popped out on my arms.

"It's coming," I whispered. "You got it."

Then—the boat stopped.

Jake pulled a little harder. The boat rocked toward us, then pulled back, making the rod bend.

I looked down the bank to make sure none of the alligators had moved closer to us. I walked off a ways so I could see around the boat. Maybe I could tell what was holding it.

"The rope's tangled in some branches," I called to Jake from down the bank. "Pull a little harder—but don't break the line."

Only Jake didn't pull. He stood there with his mouth gaping open.

"What did you say?" he asked finally.

I frowned back at him.

"I said the rope's tangled in some branches," I repeated. "Pull a little harder, but don't break the line."

But again Jake didn't pull. He kept looking at me with his mouth flopped open. Then he put the rod down. He stuck it between a couple of logs on the bank so the line was still tight. With that weird look still messing up his face, he walked over to me.

"What did you say?"

I felt one side of my upper lip curl.

"You deaf or something?" "I said the rope's tangled in . . ."

"I heard you," Jake interrupted. He looked out at our boat. "Ben . . ."

"What?"

He looked me square in the eye. There was something frightening about his stare, something cold.

"Ben," he repeated, *we didn't have a rope.*"

CHAPTER 17

"Get your foot off my hand," I growled up at Jake. He looked down between his feet at me and moved over.

"Sorry," he said.

This time, Jake had beat me to the tree. He stood on the top branch and I stood directly under him. Like a couple of baby squirrels, frightened by the crackling of a branch, we'd scurried to the safety of our tree.

But now that we were here, I felt like an idiot. I hadn't even thought about climbing up here—I just did it. We looked all around. We looked at the alligators and counted them. We looked at the pond.

But mostly, we looked for whoever had taken our boat and tied it to the brush at the far bank.

"You see anything?" Jake asked.

I shook my head. "Nothing. No boat. Nobody hiding—nobody moving around. Nothing."

"He must have come when we were digging for that dumb treasure," Jake sighed. "I'm sorry I got mad at you for not pulling the boat far enough up on the bank. You did. Somebody dragged it off and tied it on the far side of the pond, somebody who wants us to get eaten by those gators. He knew we'd swim for the boat. He knew . . ."

I looked up at him. A flake of tree bark hit my eye when he moved his foot. I blinked.

"But, who, Jake? Who'd do that to us?"

I don't know how long we stayed in the tree but, judging by the sun, it was well past three when we came down. We were both so hungry and thirsty, we simply couldn't stay in the tree any longer.

I went back and picked up the fishing rod where Jake had left it. Slowly and steadily, I started to pull. Maybe the boat would come loose. Maybe the branch our boat was tied to would break.

The rod bent double. I pulled harder. It bent more. The string was so tight when I pulled, it vibrated like the high note on a piano. There was a sudden *pop* and the line snapped. I fell backward onto the bank.

I scrambled to my feet. After I glared at the boat for a second, I reeled my line in. From my tackle box, I got two weights. I slipped them on the end of my line, then tied three three-way hooks to the end. I cast again.

Finally, after a whole bunch of casts, I dropped my weights and hooks in the back of the boat. I reeled in easy, so the hooks would hang and the weights wouldn't let my line fall in the water. When I was sure I had something solid with my hooks, I started pulling.

Again, my line snapped.

"It's not gonna work," Jake said as he watched me tie another set of weights and hooks to my broken line. "Your fishing line's not strong enough to pull the boat loose. It isn't gonna work."

I ignored him and tried again.

I reeled my broken line back across the pond. Then I threw my rod down and kicked sand at it. Jake was right. It wasn't going to work.

Three times we'd managed to hook the boat. Three times our line had broken. The boat was tied tight to that brush and not about to come loose.

I glared down at my fishing rod. The useless thing just sat there.

"Ben!"

Jake's shout startled me. I jumped.

He was pointing down the bank. One of the smaller alligators had crawled out onto our little island. He was coming toward us.

In a flash, we grabbed dead sticks and branches and

threw them at him. Our barrage filled the air. Finally, he slipped back into the water and glided off.

We watched him go, then looked around, studying the others. They were all closer. We hadn't really noticed before, although we *had* been keeping our eye on them while we tried to get the boat. They had been moving so slowly toward us, we hadn't sensed that they were closing in. It was like they were stalking their prey. Slow and easy, an inch at a time, they moved in. Closer and closer.

"That's it," Jake barked as he slung one last stick at the pond. "I'm getting out of here!"

For a moment I thought he was headed for our tree again. I followed a few yards behind him, but he marched right past the tree and headed for the back of the island.

Standing a little behind him, I watched as he studied the water. Here, it was only about ten yards or so wide. It looked shallow, too. Maybe not more than knee- to ankle-deep. Beyond the ten yards or so of water was the swamp.

He looked in both directions, checking to make sure there were no alligators in this part of the pond. Then he marched right out into the water.

I swiveled my head from side to side to make sure no gator was sneaking up on him. Part of me wanted to chase after him as he crossed the gap between our island

and the swamp. Another part of me kept my feet planted firmly on the ground.

The water looked shallow. But clear as this pond was, I wasn't sure. I held my breath and kept watching.

Jake went a ways, and only his shoes and ankles were underwater. In about the middle, he started going deeper and deeper.

He started coming up. I smiled and slapped my hands together. He stood on dry land on the other side of the shallows. With a smile that covered his whole face, he turned to me. The knees of his jeans weren't even wet.

"Come on," he waved. "Come on. Let's go."

I didn't walk across the shallow stretch of water. I looked both ways to make sure none of the gators were around, then I *ran*!

We jumped around and patted each other on the back, and headed off toward the swamp.

It was a swamp, too. There was lots of mud and even water standing in places. But there were also bushes and shrubs with dry, firm ground around where they grew. We picked our way carefully, staying on solid ground. The land stretched out like a peninsula toward our little island. In fact, the only thing that made our island an island was that short stretch of shallow water we had to cross. The pond lay on either side of where we walked and we kept an eye on it. Sure enough, one of the alligators cruised along, watching us. He kept his distance, staying well out in the water. We kept our distance, too, staying well in the middle, away from the banks.

We walked about thirty yards or so, picking our way from one clump of brush to another. On either side of us, the pond was getting smaller—like it was narrowing into two separate channels. The land where we walked seemed to be growing wider.

Then we came to a stretch of open sand. It went clear across the peninsula in both directions. The pond ended just about where the sand was.

We'd made it. There was no water or mud oozing up from the sand, so it looked firm. Now we could put some distance between us and those horrible, nasty, dangerous alligators.

Jake was a little ahead of me. We were both in a hurry to get away from the island, so he was walking pretty fast.

Suddenly, he stopped.

I stopped, too.

"Ben?"

There was an edge to his voice, a strange hint of fear when he called my name. Then he looked over his shoulder. His eyes were wide. "Ben! I'm stuck."

I started to go give him a hand, but when I tried to

walk toward him, I almost fell. My feet wouldn't move. I looked down.

The sand was over the top of my shoes. I raised my right foot so I could back up and get out of the sand. When I did, my left foot sank deeper—almost to my knee. When I tried to pull it out, my right foot went clean down, past my knee.

I blinked.

"Jake," I called. I could hear the fear in my own voice.

"Ben," he called back to me. I could hear the panic in his voice, too.

He looked over his shoulder at me. Struggling against the sand, he was clear down past both knees. I was almost up to my knees, and the harder I tried to pull free, the deeper I sank. There was panic in Jake's eyes.

"Ben!"

"Jake!"

We both called each other's name. The panic of our voices was sharp against the still, swamp air. And at the very same instant, we both shrieked:

"Quicksand!"

CHAPTER 18

The harder I yanked against the sand, the more it pulled at my feet and legs. I stopped struggling for a minute and the sand quit dragging me down. I wasn't free, but I wasn't sinking either.

I stood perfectly still and held my breath. With a shudder, I realized I was sinking. It was slow—much slower than when I struggled.

Jake had sunk almost to his waist. I tried to turn so I could lean back but my legs were covered to the middle of my thighs.

Since I couldn't turn around, I looked over my shoulder. There was a small bush. I could see my footprint in the soft dirt beside it from where I had stepped into the quicksand.

If I could only reach that bush . . .

I leaped backward and stretched. Suddenly I fell. I

almost cried out, but I didn't. When I landed on my back, I expected the sand to swallow me. It would be over then. I'd be gone—beneath the choking, shifting sand.

Only, I didn't get swallowed. I just lay there, stretched out on my back. Beneath me, I could feel the moisture of the sand through my shirt. But it held me and I didn't die—like I was sure I was going to.

Carefully, slowly, I reached out for the bush. My fingers touched the leaves. I grabbed them but they came off in my hand.

I stretched harder. I pushed the back of my head deep into the moving sand so I could look at the bush. It was upside down, but I spotted a large branch sticking out. I caught it.

"Don't break." My prayer was nothing more than a whisper. "Please, dear God, don't let it break."

Then my other hand had the branch. I started to pull.

"Ben, help me!" Jake cried. "Don't let me die. Help me!"

I couldn't see Jake because of the way I was stretched out on my back. But I could hear him again and again as he pleaded for me to help him.

It didn't take long to find that if I kicked my feet and jerked, I didn't go anyplace. The sand just kept sucking at me. But if I lay perfectly still and only pulled with my arms, I began to move.

Slowly, an inch at a time, I pulled closer and closer to firm ground. The little branch held.

It seemed like an eternity, but finally I could feel something solid beneath my shoulders. The branch I was clinging to bumped against my head. Without letting go of it, I reached back with my other hand, searching for another handhold farther up on the bank. When I found it and made sure it was sturdy, I started pulling again.

I could feel the ground beneath my back. Finally, when my bottom was scooted out on the hard surface, I let go of the bush and sat up. I pulled my legs out of the quicksand and scrambled to my feet.

My shoes were gone, but I had made it. I could hear myself panting. A little tremble swept over me. I never knew how good it felt to be free.

I looked down at where I'd been trapped in the quicksand. There was no trace of where I'd been. No print. No hole in the mud. The sand had simply flowed back in. It looked smooth and firm.

"Ben." Jake called my name. His voice was weak and faint. I looked up.

He was down to the middle of his chest. He wasn't struggling anymore. He wasn't even moving. His eyes caught mine. They seemed dull and empty.

"Tell my daddy I love him," was all he said.

CHAPTER 19

"I'll get you out, I promise."

That's what I told Jake. Only I didn't stick around to make sure I had convinced him. There wasn't time.

I wanted to run. I wanted to go tearing around to find a log or a limb—something I could hold out for him to cling to.

I didn't.

Instead, I took one step at a time. With each step, I planted my bare foot, testing the ground to make sure it was firm before I took another step.

"Hang on," I called while I looked around. "Don't move. If you move, it sucks you down. Just be real still."

From time to time, I looked across the sand at him.

Jake wasn't moving. He didn't seem to be sinking anymore. But each time I checked on him, he seemed a
little deeper in the sand. He *was* going down. But it was
so slow, it was like watching the big hand on the clock
at school. When I watched him, I couldn't tell. But
when I searched for a branch or limb, and then looked
back at him, I knew he was still being sucked down by
the quicksand.

There was nothing to throw to him. I had looked
everyplace on the little strip of swamp between the
island and the quicksand. There wasn't a stick or a
branch. All I could find were little, short twigs that
wouldn't come close to reaching my friend.

You've got to find something, I growled to myself.
Anything. You've got to help him.

My jeans had bagged down around my bottom. I
could feel the cool air on my skin. Sticking my fingers
into my belt loops, I pulled them up.

A little smile pulled at my cheeks. I felt a tingle race
up my back.

As quickly as I could, I leaped from one clump of
brush to another and made my way back to the edge of
the quicksand. There, I stripped my jeans off.

Testing the bank with my hands, I crawled as close
to the edge of the quicksand as I dared. Then, holding
one leg of my jeans, I threw the other end to Jake.

His desperate face seemed to brighten. He lunged

for it, but missed. When he jumped, he sank quickly. He was down to his shoulders.

"Don't grab at it, Jake," I ordered angrily. "Don't move. Just reach out with your hands."

I threw again. Once more, he grabbed at it. Now, only his head and the very tip of his shoulders were left above the deadly quicksand.

"I mean it, Jake," I screamed. "Don't grab! Just reach. Slow and easy."

This time, he listened. But again my throw was short. I moved out farther. My hand sank in the quicksand. I jumped back.

Just six inches, I told myself. If I just had something six inches longer . . .

I couldn't reach him. My jeans weren't long enough. And I had to hurry. He was almost down to his neck. If he didn't get hold of something—soon—it would be too late.

I dragged my jeans back across the sand and wadded them up to try another throw. I stopped. Beside me was the little bush I'd used to pull myself out. Quick as a flash, I yanked the belt off my jeans. I put it around the sturdiest branch of the bush, then buckled it in the first notch. I stuck my leg through the belt and bent it like I did when I hung from the monkey bars at school.

With my knee at the very edge of the quicksand, I leaned as far out as I could and threw.

Jake caught the other leg of my blue jeans.

"Don't pull," I screamed at him, as loud as I could. "I haven't got a very good hold. You start yanking, and we'll lose them."

Jake nodded.

I smiled, glad that he was listening to me and not still in a panic.

"You just hold onto them. Let me do all the pulling. Understand?"

He nodded again.

"I'm gonna start pulling," I said. "Don't wiggle your legs or anything. Don't *you* pull. Just sort of stretch out on your belly. Okay?"

I just had hold of my jeans' leg with the tips of my fingers and thumb. The way I had my leg hiked up, through the belt, put me in a real weird position. When I pulled, I got a cramp in my hip and side.

I kept pulling.

I wanted Jake to come slipping out, like toothpaste squirting from a tube. He didn't. In fact, nothing seemed to happen at first. I pulled. Jake hung on, as I told him to, but he didn't move.

I didn't yank or jerk. I just kept pulling. The cramp in my hip hurt something terrible. I loosened my grip on the jeans and scooted my hand up. Now I had a better hold on them.

Jake *was* closer.

The cramp finally brought tears to my eyes. I could hardly stand it. Still, I kept my steady pull on the jeans.

It took forever, but finally Jake was lying on top of the sand. I could see his bottom as he lay, facedown coming toward me one *slow* inch at a time.

"Don't move," I said. "I've got to get a better hold."

I pulled myself backward with my knee that was hooked through the belt. When I changed positions, the cramp grabbed my hip and side. I wanted to scream. Instead, I sort of fell back into the bush. My leg wouldn't move, but now I could get hold of the jeans with both hands. I started pulling again.

I don't know how long it took. I do know that it was almost dark when Jake reached out and grabbed my ankle with both hands. He grunted and groaned as he slid himself out onto firm ground.

I fell back into the bush. I didn't notice the branches sticking me. I was too tired.

Breathing hard and exhausted, we just lay there for a long, long time. After a while, I rubbed at the cramp in my hip and tried to straighten my leg. I couldn't move it. I wiped the water from my eyes and tried it again.

Jake finally made it to his hands and knees. He didn't go any farther, though. He just stayed there on all fours. Finally, he looked up at me.

"Thanks." He reached out and patted my leg. "Thanks, Ben."

I tried to smile, but even my face hurt because I was so tired. All I could do was nod and keep working at the cramp in my hip.

Jake got to his feet. He still clutched the leg of my jeans. His hand shook. His knuckles were white and he had to use his other hand to pry the jeans' leg loose. He handed me my jeans, then reached out to help me up.

It hurt when I stood, but the terrible, agonizing cramp started to go away.

"We've got to get back to the island," Jake said softly. "It's almost dark."

I groaned when I tried to take a step with my sore leg.

"Give me a second," I said, rubbing my hip. "I've got a cramp. Bad one. I'm not sure I can walk."

Jake nodded. Then he looked around.

"We can't stay here. There're no trees to climb. There isn't even a stick to throw if those gators come here after us. We've got to get back to the island before it gets dark. Maybe we can build a fire." His voice seemed to lighten. "Yeah," he agreed with himself, "we've got those matches in the tackle box. We'll build a fire."

He took my arm and put it over his shoulder so I could lean on him. We started toward the island.

I could almost walk normally by the time we got to

the edge of the shallows. Taking a deep breath, I stretched and rubbed my hip.

"Maybe somebody will see the fire," I said. "If we don't show up at home pretty soon, they're gonna be looking for us. Maybe if we make a big enough fire . . ."

"Can you run?" Jake cut me off.

I shifted my weight from one leg to the other, testing my sore hip. "I'm not sure. Think so."

With a nod of his head, he motioned to the bank of the shallow channel. One of the bigger alligators had swum up there. He lay completely motionless about thirty yards from where we had to cross.

Jake got a good hold of my arm. "I'll count to three, then we'll take off."

I bit my lip and nodded.

"One, two, *three!*"

We tore out across the narrow shallows as hard as we could. It amazed and terrified me—how quickly the big alligator moved. With one sweep of his enormous tail, he shot through the water like a rocket. We were far up on the bank before we stopped running and turned to look back.

The gator was where we had been just seconds ago. He floated in the narrow water. Beneath him, we could see where we'd stirred up the dirt and mud from the bottom.

"You stinking . . ." Jake gulped. He let go of me and

started chunking sticks at the monster. I found a couple of rocks beside me and pelted the gator with them.

He lay there a moment, watching us. Then, with one gentle sweep of his tail, he glided across the shallows and into the pond on the far side.

There was barely enough light left to see. We grabbed the tackle box and took it to the tree. We piled up some dry grass and brush and tried to light it.

The matches didn't work. They were too old even to strike. So Jake and I climbed up the tree.

A tree is about the worst place in the world to spend a night. And that night turned out to be the most terrifying one of my life.

That night was horrible and terrifying, but not because we were stuck in a tree with no place to lie down. And not because we were so uncomfortable we had to stay awake all night. And it wasn't because we were starving and thirstier than we'd ever been. We hadn't had a single thing to eat or drink since breakfast. It wasn't even because we were surrounded by alligators on one side and quicksand on the other and hordes of mosquitoes that hummed around our heads and bit us again and again.

All that was bad enough.

What made the night so terrifying was the man who came. The man who was trying to kill us.

CHAPTER 20

We tried sitting on the branches, only they were too narrow. They hurt our bottom or legs and it was almost impossible to keep our balance.

We finally ended up standing. We both stood on the same limb and draped our arms across one another. When one of us would start getting real sleepy or wobbly, the other would nudge him.

The moon was only about half full. The way it reflected off the smooth surface of the pond, I could still see. Not much, but some. Every now and then, one of the alligators would come floating through the places where the moonlight danced on the water. I could see them glide through the little silvery path, barely rippling the surface as they slid along.

*   *   *

I don't know when he came. My guess is that it was well after midnight.

My mouth was so dry, I felt like I'd been chewing the cotton balls that Mama used to clean off her fingernail polish. I fanned the mosquitoes away from my eyes with a wave of my hand. My eyes burned. I closed them awhile to let the pain of staying awake go away, then opened them again. I closed them once more, then heard a soft *clunk* sound. I blinked and rubbed away the sore gritty feeling.

At first I didn't see anything, but I heard the sound of splashing water. It, like the *clunk* sound, was soft and faint.

Then I saw it. A boat. It was a small boat. I could barely make it out in the dim light from the moon. There was a man in it. At least, I think there was a man. All I really saw was a dark form—a shape.

I squinted, straining my eyes against the darkness.

"Jake," I whispered. "Jake? Do you see him?"

"Yes."

Beside me, I could feel Jake straighten up. "I told you someone'd come looking for us," he said lightly. "I told you, didn't I?"

He started to jump up and down on the branch.

"Hey," he shouted, "we're up here. On the island. Help us. We're up here!"

I could just barely see, but the form in the boat put his paddle in the water. The boat stopped.

Jake kept yelling, but when there was no answer from the man, he quit. It was an eerie feeling. We held our breath and watched.

For a long time, the boat just sat there, motionless. It was so dark, the form in the boat had no face. He was just a shape—a shape that *hadn't* come to help us. Whatever, whoever—he wasn't there to rescue us.

I wanted to yell at the man. I wanted to scream for him not to go away—not to leave us here. I didn't. I knew Jake felt the same way, but neither of us made a sound. We just watched as the silent, dark form glided back to the edge of the pond and slipped into the channel that led back toward the river.

"Why would somebody want to do this to us?" I wondered out loud, trying to keep both of us awake. "Why would somebody swipe our boat? Who would want to hurt us? We haven't ever done anything bad to anybody."

Jake didn't answer. He only shook his head.

By morning, thoughts were still racing through my head. But nothing made any sense. The man who came in the boat *had* to be the same one who moved our boat. He must have known that one or both of us would try to swim after it and when we did, the alligators would come after us. The only reason he had come last night, hidden by the dark, was to see if we were still alive.

But why? Who?

Jake and I had never hurt anybody. We didn't have any enemies, not even at school. Why would somebody want to hurt us? Maybe it was the map. Maybe that man knew there was a treasure around here and he knew we had the map. But how?

I yawned so wide my jaw made a little popping sound. I rubbed my eyes, noticing the faint glow in the eastern sky. It was nearly sunrise. If we could just make it until daylight, we could get down from the tree. One of us could stand watch while the other slept. I yawned again.

"Jake?"

The branch I was standing on jerked. Jake grabbed at the limb.

"Huh," his sleepy voice moaned.

"You okay?"

"Um-hum," he answered. "You?"

I shrugged. "I'm scared."

"Me, too."

The sky was lighter now, but I still couldn't see.

"I wish we'd never found that boat or that map," Jake said, slapping at a mosquito. He was more awake now. "It's like the whole thing was a big trap. There's probably not even a treasure. It's like somebody arranged this whole thing—the boat, the map, the fence—everything just to get us trapped here."

"Why?" I asked.

Jake yawned. "Maybe he wasn't after us. Maybe somebody else was supposed to find the boat and the map. Remember that day I took you to see it for the first time? Somebody had tried to hide it. Remember the wet sand?"

"I remember."

"Maybe somebody else was supposed to find the boat. Whoever's doing this probably wasn't after us at all. But since we found the place and the alligators, the person figures he's got to get rid of us or we'll tell. Whoever he is was trying to get rid of somebody else and we just stumbled into his trap."

The sun still wasn't up, but there was more light. I could make out some of the larger trees in the swamp. The banks of the pond were starting to take shape. I thought I could see the biggest alligator floating around near our boat.

"Remember the alligators we saw in Daddy's truck?"

Jake nodded.

"Those were teeny-tiny compared to these. I bet these alligators have been here a long time."

Jake nodded again. "I bet if your dad knew what those alligators were going to look like when they grew up, he would never have helped the game ranger bring them in." Jake frowned. "You don't think your dad knows anything about these alligators, do you?"

I shook my head. "No. He kept talking about how there weren't any alligators. If he'd known about these . . ."

"Somebody knew about them." Jake cut me off. "The fence we found—remember we hauled our boat over it? It was made out of cattle panels and logs were piled on it."

"Yeah."

"That's what the fence was for. Not to keep people out, but to keep these alligators in. That fence has been there a long, long time. There was mud and dirt on the logs and there were places where weeds and stuff were growing around it. On the other hand, if somebody was making a trap to kill somebody, he made it a long time ago."

I frowned, watching the big gator work his way closer to our boat.

"But why would somebody go to all this trouble to kill somebody? Why not just shoot 'em or stab 'em with a knife or something?"

Jake shook his head. "The police can check the bullet that comes out of a gun to tell where it came from. If somebody stabs somebody, the murderer has to be present to do it and might be seen. On the other hand, if alligators or quicksand kill somebody, there's no evidence. If you sink in quicksand, there's nothing left. And if one of those alligators ever got hold of you, by the time he was done, can you imagine what . . ."

A loud *thud* came from across the pond. Jake and I instantly fell silent, afraid the man in the boat had come back. My fingers tightened around the branch.

I squinted, searching for what had made the sound. It came again. There was enough light from the rising sun so that I could see.

When the sound came a third time, I found out what was making it. It was the big gator I had seen by our boat.

He bumped the boat a couple more times with his nose. Then he rose out of the water. His long, warty snout slammed down on the boat's side, making it rock. He hit it again and water started rushing in.

"He's after our food," Jake cried.

Now the alligator had his front feet on the side of the boat. More water rushed in, and the boat and gator, both, went under.

"That's our food," Jake yelled. "He can't have it. It's ours. It's our boat . . . I'm gonna . . ."

Jake let go of the limb with one hand. He started to swing to the next limb and climb down from the tree. I didn't know what he was going to do—maybe throw rocks and sticks at the big gator. But whatever it was, it didn't matter, because just as Jake let go of the bottom limb, I reached down and grabbed him by the hair.

"Hey," he squawked, "what the . . ."

I strained, pulling him back up on the branch with me.

"You trying to yank my hair out? Let go!"

When I had him back to the limb, I let go of his hair and pointed.

One of the alligators was on our island. Quiet and still, he lay like an old, rotted log—not six feet away from our tree.

CHAPTER 21

We waited in the tree until it was completely light. By then we were both so mad we could hardly see straight. We had gone all night without one bit of sleep. We were both about to starve, too. And that stinking, big gator had sunk our boat to get the sandwiches out of the sack that Jake had packed. And now, three of the alligators were moving around on our island. They were like a pack of coonhounds who had treed a raccoon and were moving in for the kill.

I nudged Jake with my elbow. "Let's go."

He shook his head. I nudged him again. "Come on. We can pelt 'em with sticks and rocks and stuff and run 'em off."

Jake only shook his head again. I looked at him. There

137

were dark circles under his eyes from lack of sleep.

"It's no use," he said. "If we run 'em off, they'll only come back. They just keep waiting. It's hopeless."

"Somebody will find us," I said. "They're bound to be looking for us. All we have to do is hang on."

Jake only shook his head. "We're getting weak from no food and no water. I'm so tired and sleepy . . . I don't even care anymore." He sighed. "It's hopeless."

The air whooshed out of my chest, and my shoulders sagged. Jake was right. It *was* hopeless. We couldn't swim for safety. The alligators would get us for sure in the water. We couldn't get off the back of the island. That was covered with quicksand—and there was probably even more farther out in the swamp. We couldn't even stay up here in the tree. If we did, sooner or later, we'd be so tired from going without sleep, or so weak from lack of food and water, that we'd pass out and fall. When that happened, if the fall didn't break our necks, the gators would get us. I just wanted to cry.

Instead, I smiled.

It was the first time I'd smiled since we had come to the island. *But, I smiled.* It was a big, sneaky, broad smile that stretched clear across my face.

Jake glanced at me with his sad eyes. He frowned. "What's wrong with you?" he asked.

My smile got even bigger. "That gator down there."

I pointed at the one closest to the tree. "He's wantin' to eat us, right?"

Jake tilted his head to the side, but didn't answer.

I nodded, answering myself. "Well, I've got a surprise for him."

"What?" Jake asked.

"He's not gonna eat us. *We're* gonna eat him."

The alligator didn't even blink when we climbed down from the tree. He lay there frozen—trying to act like a dead log until one of us came close enough for him to snatch in his jaws. Only, we didn't get close.

Instead, we went after the other two gators that had invaded our little island. We threw sticks and rocks at them. It took a long time, but we finally ran both of them into the water.

We looked back at the one closest to the tree. He still lay there, waiting—thinking we hadn't seen him.

The two gators we chased off glided across the pond to the safety of the far side. We looked around, making sure none of the others were close. Across the pond, our boat had come back up. The edges were just above the surface. There was Styrofoam or something under the seats so it couldn't sink. But being full of water, it wouldn't float either. Beside it, the paper sack that Jake had packed our food in floated, empty.

Jake and I looked back at the alligator by the tree. Then we looked at each other.

"Let's go get him!"

We picked up long sticks and rocks. I found a couple of sticks that were slender and straight, like spears. On the way across the island, I broke the ends so they'd have sharp points.

When we got to the gator, we eased up as close as we dared, then we let him have it with everything we had. Our sticks and rocks bounced off his tough hide. He turned his head and snapped at us when one of the rocks or sticks hit a place that hurt. I threw my spears, but they only glanced across his back and slid into the sand.

Then, suddenly, he took off. He rose up on his stubby, little legs and headed for the side of the island.

"He's getting away," Jake screamed. "If he gets to the water, we'll lose him."

The alligator was ten times slower on the land than he was in the water. Still, he moved so fast that it surprised me. His body and tail swayed from side to side as his short legs raced for the safety of the pond.

Jake managed to outrun him. On the little hill near the bank, Jake picked up a club and jumped right in front of the thing. Then he brought his club down and clunked the gator square in the middle of his head.

The alligator stopped. He opened his mouth as wide as he could. A loud, threatening, hissing sound shook the still air. When his jaws snapped shut, the crack sounded like a gunshot.

Jake bopped him again.

By then I managed to catch up with him. The limb I'd picked up wasn't as heavy as the one Jake had, but it was longer. I clubbed the alligator, too.

He hissed again and snapped at us with his steel-trap jaws a few times. Then he started backing up. He made a run to the side, trying to get around us and back to the water. Again, we headed him off.

"The pit," Jake called to me, once we had the gator stopped.

"What?"

Jake pointed to the middle of our island. "The pit. Where we were digging for treasure. If we can get him in that, he can't get out."

It took us most of the morning. We chunked sticks and rocks at him and poked him with poles. He'd move a ways, stop to fight us, then make a run for the pond. We'd stop him and start our routine of chunking and poking him again. Finally, though, we managed to herd the savage monster to the center of the little island. But at the edge of the pit, he stopped. No matter how much throwing or poking or jabbing we did, he wouldn't go in.

A few feet away, I saw a fallen tree. I grabbed it. The thing was so long and heavy, I couldn't pick it up, so I dragged it over to the pit. When Jake figured out what I was doing, he rushed to help.

Like ancient knights using a battering ram against a castle gate, we charged the alligator. Jake was in front. He planted the root end of the tree against the gator's side.

The scaly monster lurched sideways. His ferocious jaws clamped shut on the wood. Jake scooted back toward my end of the tree. Then, digging our feet into the sand and pushing with all our might, we shoved the tree and the alligator into the treasure pit.

He landed on his back. Snapping those fierce jaws and thrashing his powerful tail, he tried to flip over. But somehow, the way the tree was across his chest, he couldn't manage.

In a flash, Jake and I grabbed our shovels. We raced to the edge of the pit and attacked. We jabbed the sharp, metal edges at him again and again. We aimed for the soft, white part of his belly and the soft, loose skin at his neck.

He thrashed and fought for survival. The thick hide

at his throat gave. Blood came. I felt my shovel strike, and sink into the soft part of his stomach.

What we did was brutal. It was nasty and cruel and ugly. But finally he was dead—and we were alive—and that's what really mattered.

CHAPTER 22

Exhausted, we collapsed beside the pit. We lay there for a long time, gasping for air. Now and then we'd take turns rising up on one elbow to make sure none of the other alligators had come back to our island. The sweat rolled off my face and arms and chest, but I was too tired even to wipe it away. My mouth was so dry, I couldn't swallow.

As I lay there, trying to recover from the battle with the alligator, I couldn't help thinking about last year when we studied prehistoric man in school. I remembered Mrs. Parks talking about how the cavemen would attack animals with nothing but rocks and sharp sticks or stone axes. I remembered picturing it in my mind's eye. In the safety of our warm classroom, I could almost

144

see the men in their animal-skin clothes. I could see them fighting those huge monsters—stabbing, throwing. As she talked, I could imagine one man being gored by a huge buffalo or trampled by a woolly mammoth. I could see another thrown fifty yards by one swoosh of its powerful tusks.

"It's a wonder the human race survived," Mrs. Parks said.

I rose up on one elbow. Jake lay a few feet away, still clutching his shovel like a spear. The alligator lay lifeless and bloody at the bottom of the pit.

"It's a wonder *we* survived," I repeated, remembering Mrs. Parks's words.

But we had. A weird feeling caught hold of me. A strange feeling, down deep inside. A feeling of something very, very old—primitive. I was weak and exhausted, but for some reason, I felt powerful and strong.

Jake and I had faced our monster. Jake and I had survived.

It took us a long time before we had enough strength to sit up. I struggled to my feet and went to the edge of the pond. Jake followed.

We knew that drinking pond water was dangerous. We knew we'd probably catch something and end up really sick, but we didn't care. We either had to drink something or we'd die. Jake stood watch for gators while I drank, then I watched for him.

When we were full, I went to the tree where we'd left my tackle box. I came back with it and got out the knife we used for scaling fish. Jake poked the gator a couple more times with his shovel. When we were positive he was dead, we took the knife and crawled down into the pit.

"We've got him," Jake said. "Now what are we gonna do with him?"

"We're gonna skin him like a catfish," I said confidently. "Daddy says that down in Louisiana and Mississippi, folks eat alligator tail all the time. He says it's really good eating. Let's see if we can cut off the tail."

The gator's hide was tough, but taking turns with the knife, we finally managed to get through it. We cut a circle around his whole tail, then pulled and pried and tugged until the hide started tearing.

It kind of peeled off, like Mama's stockings when she pulled them down—only not nearly as easy. Our fingers ached and we were tired, but just a little of the meat showed under the skin. It was white, like a chicken breast or frog leg frying in a pan.

Jake took my knife and cut off a strip of meat. He halved it and handed me part. We were both starving, so I poked it into my mouth and started chewing.

Almost instantly, my nose crinkled up and I gagged.

It was like chewing on a dead fish.

I spit it out.

Jake did the same. He spit a few more times, trying to get the taste out of his mouth. Then he wiped his lips with the tail of his T-shirt.

"I can't take that," he said. "We're gonna have to build a fire."

I shook my head. "The matches don't work. Remember?"

He nodded. "We'll have to do it like they showed us in Boy Scouts. You know, like the Indians did—with a bow and a pointed stick."

I could remember seeing the picture in the Boy Scout manual. It was called a bow-and-drill. First off, we needed a straight stick with a pointed end.

That was no problem. We had plenty of sticks and we sharpened the end of one with our knife.

Next, we had to find a limber stick to which we could tie a string or leather strap to make the bow. Jake took care of that. He scampered up our tree and cut off a green limb, about as big around as my thumb. By tearing the hem off the bottom of his T-shirt, then bending the little limb, we tied both ends to make a thing like a miniature Indian bow.

We found a flat piece of wood and laid it on the ground. With our hands we smashed up little pieces of dead grass and tiny, dry twigs into a mixture that we laid in a pile in the middle of the wood. Jake put the point of the straight stick into the center of the mound and used the palm of his hand at the top of the stick to hold it straight up and down. Then he took the bow and twisted the bowstring in such a way that the string looped around the stick.

By pulling the bow back and forth, like someone playing a bass fiddle, the point of the straight stick began spinning round and round in the kindling mixture. Jake moved the bow back and forth as fast as he could.

The only trouble was, the palm of his hand got hot faster than the mixture of kindling that was supposed to catch on fire.

We found a block of wood to help hold down the top of the stick.

When Jake got tired from moving the bow back and forth, I switched places with him. All we had to do was keep moving the bow fast enough and long enough so the spinning of the pointed straight stick would cause enough friction and heat to ignite our kindling.

"It's not going to work," I told Jake after we had switched places about three times. "Remember, we tried this at the Boy Scout meeting. We finally had to use Mr. Byner's matches."

Jake gently shoved me out of the way and took my

place with the bow-and-drill. His bottom jaw seemed to stick way out. "That was different," he explained. "At the Boy Scout meeting, we didn't *have* to start a fire. There was someone there to help, if it didn't work. Here—if we don't start a fire, we're gonna starve. It *will* make the difference."

We kept moving the bow back and forth until I thought my arm was going to drop off. We switched places so many times I got dizzy. We worked and worked and worked—forever. Nothing happened.

Then—at long last—a little wisp of smoke rose from the dry powder. Jake blew ever so gently. A small flame, almost blue at first, crackled and sputtered.

We were quick, but real careful, to add more kindling. The flame was so small that even a leaf could have knocked it out. We added grass and the powder that we'd crumbled up from dead sticks. Finally, when we had our little fire burning enough to put sticks the size of our finger on it, we jumped up and laughed and cheered and patted each other on the back.

It took forever to get the fire started, but once it was going, it took us only minutes to pile the wood on it. We had a small but roaring blaze.

Jake kept an eye on the fire. I took the knife and went back to our tree. There, I cut off a couple of branches. They were thin and about two feet long. I whittled points on both ends. Jake kept adding wood to the fire.

I took the sticks with me and crawled into the pit. I cut four chunks of meat from the alligator's tail. They were about as big around as my fist. I threaded two onto the end of each stick, then went back to the fire.

Jake had a good blaze going now. Some of the sticks in the middle were already turning to red-hot coals. I put the other pointed ends of the sticks in the ground so that the meat could hang over the fire and cook. Only, the limbs were too limber or the meat was too heavy, so I had to take two off and only leave one piece of meat on the end of each stick.

Now all we had to do was wait for our alligator to cook. Jake reached down and got the two pieces of meat I'd taken off the sticks. He smiled and pitched them right into the middle of our fire.

"I'm starving," he said. "A few ashes and dirt never hurt anybody."

We piled more wood on the fire. Then we went and gathered some more. The one thing there was plenty of on the island was wood. It took us only minutes to stack a pile close to the fire, almost as tall as we were.

I twisted the sticks so the meat would cook evenly.

"Soon as we're through eating," Jake said, "let's light the whole pile. Somebody's bound to be searching for us by now. Maybe they'll see the fire."

I nodded. "Yeah. And let's get some green stuff, too.

Green leaves make lots of smoke. Maybe somebody'll see it."

We attacked every little bush on the island and piled up green wood and twigs beside our fire. Then we climbed the tree and practically stripped it of every green branch.

By the time we had all our wood gathered, the alligator meat smelled *wonderful*. Jake took a sharp stick and speared the two chunks he'd thrown into the fire. After he let them cool for a little bit, he dusted off the ashes and used the knife to cut away the black stuff on the outside.

I hadn't realized how hungry I was. That black, crusty, burned alligator meat was the best thing I ever tasted. We gobbled both pieces down in no time, so we got the other two pieces off the end of the sticks and ate them.

My stomach growled and fussed at me. We cut two more pieces of alligator tail and put them on our sticks to roast.

We sat back and rested a moment. We patted our stomachs and licked our lips. Jake pulled a stick with a flame on the end of it from the fire and lit the big pile we'd stacked nearby.

In a little bit, the flames roared so high and hot, we had to move back.

Somebody was bound to see the smoke. People were surely out looking for us. Neither Jake nor I had *ever* been gone a whole night without telling somebody. They'd find us. They'd come.

Nobody came.

CHAPTER 23

It was the morning of our third day on the island. Still, nobody came.

Just before dark we had gone to the edge of the pond. We scooped up handfuls of mud from the bank and rubbed it onto each other. Being covered with mud and staying in the smoke from our fire seemed to help keep the mosquitoes off.

We slept better that night. One of us added wood to the fire while the other rested. When he was so sleepy he couldn't hold his head up, he'd wake the other. When light came, we ate more of our alligator for breakfast. Our gator was starting to stink. It wasn't bad, yet, but we knew this was about the last time we could eat any of it before it spoiled. So we cooked and ate some more, then drank again from the pond.

Since we'd made the fire, the alligators had stayed off our island. They just floated around the pond—waiting.

Jake told me that during the night, when I was asleep, the man in the boat had come back. He said that even with the fire, he could barely see him.

"Did he do anything? Say anything?"

Jake shook his head.

"He just watched, then slid away into the dark."

A gulping sound came from my throat when I swallowed. "He's just waiting. He's waiting for the alligators to get us or for us to starve to death."

Jake smiled real big. "We fooled him. We're not gonna starve to death." He burped and rubbed his stomach. "I'm almost starting to like alligator tail."

I gave a half-smile and shrugged. "What if that guy gets tired of waiting?"

Jake looked at me. His eyes seemed sad and tired. "What do you mean?"

"I mean, what if he decides we're not going to starve and the alligators aren't going to get us? What if he comes with a gun? What if he comes tonight and throws us out in the pond?"

It was one of those questions that, the moment I asked it, I wished I hadn't.

Jake didn't answer. He walked back and threw some

more wood on the fire. We sat down and did nothing but stare at the flames for a long, long time.

After a while, Jake picked up a long, fat stick and started pounding it against the palm of his hand like a club. "I hope he does come," Jake growled. "I'll bash him in the head, then we'll take the boat and leave him here for the alligators."

"But, if he's got a gun . . . ," I mumbled, "we'd never get close enough to hit him."

We sat and stared at the flames again.

It was noon before we finally got tired of sitting and thinking.

Jake took a long stick and waded across the shallows at the back of the island. I stood watch for alligators while he worked along the edge of the quicksand. He poked the stick in almost every inch of ground, trying to find some solid land where we could walk out.

There was nothing but quicksand. After more than an hour, he slammed the stick to the ground and went back to the fire.

"They're not gonna find us," he moaned, plopping down in the sand. "Nobody's ever gonna find us."

"They'll find us," I snapped.

Jake crossed his legs. He propped his elbows on his knees and held his chin in his hands. He didn't say any more.

I felt sorry for myself. But mostly, I felt sorry for Mama. She had probably worried herself half to death about me. She and Grandma and Daddy . . . how would they feel if nobody ever found us?

Around noontime, we piled up more wood for the night and ate more alligator. We wondered why no one had found us. Maybe they weren't looking. We'd been gone three days. Maybe they figured our boat had sunk on the river and that we'd drowned. Maybe they were looking for us way upstream or down by Jacob's Bend.

Maybe they thought we ran away from home, and they were waiting for us to come back. What if they weren't even looking for us? What if they didn't find us? . . .

Jake went back for another helping of alligator tail. I sat staring at the fire.

"*Ben!!!*"

Jake's scream startled me. I jumped and almost fell over backward. Blinking, I looked around. He was standing by the pit where we had killed the alligator.

"Ben!" He yelled my name again.

I grabbed the shovel beside me and raced toward him.

I don't know what I was expecting to see—maybe another alligator trapped in our pit. Maybe another boat buried in the sand—I didn't know.

What I *did* see when I rushed up beside Jake was . . . nothing!

Jake stood there, looking at the carcass of the dead alligator.

"What is it?" I asked nervously. "What is it, Jake."

He pointed down at the pit. I could still see nothing but the dead alligator.

"What?" I demanded.

Jake jabbed a finger at the pit. "There," he smiled. "The pit. We'll cover it with brush. When the guy comes tonight and can't see us, he'll crawl up on the island to look around. Then he'll fall into the pit."

We worked like madmen. We spent the next couple of hours digging the pit deeper and deeper. We made the sides as smooth as we could with the edges of our shovels. When it was finally deep enough so Jake had to get on my shoulders to get out, he pulled me up after him and we started gathering stuff to cover it with.

That was where the problem came in. The whole island was covered with dead sticks and limbs, but the only thing long enough to cover the pit was too thick and heavy to collapse under anyone's weight. We climbed up the tree and cut off branches. They were thin and limber, but since the tree branches were the only thing green on the whole entire island, they stuck out like a sore thumb. Even at night, a blindman could almost see that the branches were covering up something.

Our plan for making a trap out of the pit simply wouldn't work.

We went back and sat down by the fire.

I tugged at my earlobe and looked around at all the dead trees and limbs and sticks. But we couldn't make a raft—we didn't have anything to tie it together with.

A bridge might work, only the logs would never float if we stepped on them and—like the raft, there was nothing to hold them together.

I don't know how long I sat, staring out at the water. When I turned back to Jake, he was gone. The air caught in my throat. I looked around frantically, trying to find him.

I sighed. Jake had been there all along. He had just moved a few yards and lain very still. Being covered with mud to keep the mosquitoes off, he had been hard to see at first.

I blinked a couple of times. I sat up so quickly and so straight, my back made a little popping sound. I leaped to my feet and looked at the channel that separated our island from Quicksand Swamp. I thought about logs and Jake—all covered with mud, and quicksand, and . . .

I smiled so wide it almost hurt.

"I've got it, Jake. I know how we can trap that guy!"

CHAPTER 24

"A bridge," I gasped.

Jake tilted his head, and nodded.

"Yeah, we could sure use a bridge."

I started jumping up and down.

"No, not *use* a bridge," I explained. "We'll *build* a bridge."

Jake stared at me. His mouth fell open and his eyes crossed. Then he sort of laughed.

"The alligators are gonna love that! I'll help you build it, but the minute you try walking on those dead sticks and logs—you're gonna be feeding the alligators."

I shook my head frantically.

"No, not across the pond. Across the quicksand."

Jake's eyes rolled up in his head.

"That'll work great. The logs will stay on top of the quicksand, but the second we step on one of them, they'll sink."

I smiled. "I know! But that guy in the canoe doesn't know. If he doesn't see us, he'll come to find out what happened to us, right?"

Jake nodded.

"He'll see the string of logs we laid out across the quicksand, like a bridge, and think we used that to escape. Right?"

Jake shrugged.

"When he comes to look at the bridge, we'll trap him."

Jake leaned back and tilted his head to the side.

"Trap him?"

"Yeah." I smiled again. "Come on, I'll show you."

It took a considerable amount of arguing and pulling on Jake's arm to finally get him off his bottom and onto his feet. We found the biggest log we could carry and dragged it to the edge of the little channel that separated the island from Quicksand Swamp. We went back for another and another and another.

Then we threw sticks and rocks at the lone alligator who was closest to the channel. When he left, we began carrying the logs across. It didn't take long to figure out that if one of us stood on one bank, and the other waited on the far side, we could float the logs across the narrow stretch of water a lot faster than we could carry them.

I raced across the shallows. Jake would slip a log into the water from the island and shove. When it floated to me, I'd drag it out and go back for the next. After all the logs were on my side, I watched for alligators while Jake came to join me.

We carried the logs to the edge of the quicksand, and there we laid them gently into the oozy, brown stuff. By lining up the end of the log in the quicksand with the end of the log we had on the bank, we could shove each one farther and farther out into the swamp. It took about ten logs before our chain stretched across the quicksand.

"You know," Jake said, "it looks like it just might work."

With that, he stepped out on the closest log. Just as I'd figured, it tipped and started to sink. Jake leaped back to solid ground.

My tongue traced a path across my smiling lips. "He'll test it, just like you did," I said. "When he does, he'll be off balance."

I got Jake to help me. We found a pole that was about nine feet long and not too big around. I had Jake sit down on the bank, next to me, and we held the log between us—I had to make sure we could lift it and use it like a giant spear. I grinned, knowing we could hold the log and move it around. When I looked at Jake, he wasn't smiling.

"It's almost dark," he said. "Let's get back and put a little more wood on the fire."

I shook my head. "We've got to let it burn out."

Jake's eyes got wide. "No way, man. Not after all the trouble we had getting the thing started."

"We've got to," I insisted. "If the fire is still burning, he'll know we're still around. We've got to let it go out. That guy in the canoe has got to think we crossed this bridge we built." I tugged at his arm. "We do have to go back after the shovels. We need to hurry, too. It's almost dark and we have to dig our holes and get the shovels back while there's still enough light."

Jake balked.

"What holes? What are you gonna do, Ben?"

I yanked his arm. "Come on. I'll tell you my plan while we're getting the shovels."

On the island, we took what was left of our dead alligator and threw it in the pond. The smell was terrible. I gagged a couple of times and thought I was going to throw up. But we managed to get it to the pond—as far away from the quicksand as we could. I wanted the other alligators busy with something besides us.

"What are we gonna do, Ben?" Jake insisted.

"I'll tell you in a minute."

Jake grabbed my arm. He squeezed really tight. "No, *now!*"

"The guy is gonna come tonight. When he sees that the fire is out, he'll start looking for us. When he finds the bridge across the quicksand, he'll step on that log, just like you did, and get off balance. We're gonna be hiding near the swamp. When he gets off balance, we're gonna shove him in the quicksand."

Jake stood, staring at me with his mouth gaping open. Finally, it snapped shut with a loud pop. He shook his head, as if he were dizzy or something.

"Sure," he scoffed, "we'll crouch down behind a twig or a leaf and jump up and say '*Boo*' and he'll fall in the quicksand. Yeah, man! Great plan!"

He shook his head again and turned to go add more wood to the fire. "We can't hide by the quicksand. There's nothing to hide behind. He'll see us for sure."

"No he won't!" I grabbed a shovel in one hand and caught hold of Jake's arm with the other. "I got the idea when I saw you lying down, covered up with mud to keep the mosquitoes off. We can hide right there on the bank, and he'll never see us. Now, come on."

CHAPTER 25

All the logs we had dragged to the edge of the quicksand had left a little path in the dirt. We put the nine-foot pole we had found a short distance from the path and the quicksand. In the dirt, on either side of the pole, I dug two shallow holes. We put the shovel back on the island, made sure there were no alligators around, and started covering ourselves with mud from the edge of the pond.

Just before dark, I buried Jake.

I had him lie down on the left side of the log. I shoved the dirt I had dug from the hole over him, leaving only his eyes and nose sticking out. Next, I sprinkled some dead grass and leaves over him.

I sat in the hole on the right side of the log. Using my

hands, I scraped dirt over my legs and lap, then I lay down and scooped it over my chest and stomach.

Finally, lying flat on my back, I scooped the dirt around my face and head and put a small branch over my face. Then I put my arms along my sides and tried to wiggle them down into the loose dirt.

It was the most frightening, most terrifying night I have ever spent. There was nothing around us but the darkness. That and the sounds of the swamp. Any second, I expected a snake to come slithering across my face. My eyes darted from side to side, but I didn't dare lift my head.

We didn't talk. We didn't even breathe deeply. We just lay there, frozen. The dirt felt warm. If I frowned or smiled or even blinked my eyes, the dried mud on my face would crack and pull at my skin. The air on my face was cool. Every now and then a little wisp of breeze would come. The leaves on the branch covering my face would wiggle and tickle my nose. With my arms buried at my sides, I couldn't scratch.

A spider came, once. He was little, but creepy and crawlie, like spiders are. I hated spiders. I wanted to jump up and scream and smash him with my hand. I didn't. I stuck out my bottom lip and blew. The air shook him, but he didn't leave. I blew at him again, and he went away.

The not moving was the hardest part. The quiet, the stillness, the having to lie there and never ever move— not even the tiniest little wiggle. I'd never been so still for so long in my whole entire life. I don't know where the courage came from.

It was almost morning when he came.

We didn't sit up to look, but we knew he was there because we could hear the familiar *clunk* sound that the paddle made when it bumped the side of his canoe.

Without ever looking—without ever raising our heads—we knew *he* was out there.

A million times that night I wanted to jump up and run back to the safety of the tree.

I didn't.

When the sun finally began coming up, I was so glad to see the light. But when the light came—so did the man.

I heard the sound of his footsteps as he sloshed across the shallows between the island and Quicksand Swamp. I heard a twig snap beneath his feet. Then another. And, as he got closer, I could even hear the sound of his shoes crunching in the dirt. One step at a time. One *slow, careful* step at a time, coming closer and closer and closer.

Out of the corner of my eye, I could see a boot. Above

it, blue jeans, a shirt. But I still couldn't see the face hidden in the shadow of twilight and the man's hat.

The boot came closer. One more step. It was right beside my face now. Only a few inches away. Then—he stopped.

I closed my eyes—squeezed them shut as tight as I could. I just knew he saw me. He couldn't be that close and not see. It was all over!

But he took another step. Then another.

I held my breath. Opened my eyes.

Now I could see his back. He stood, looking out at the bridge. There was a rifle in his hand. He was a tall man. He had on a cowboy hat and a red plaid shirt. He moved closer to our bridge.

I never made the slightest sound, but inside my head I was screaming, "Go on. Try it! Don't just stand there. Go on!"

Then, ever so cautiously, he put a foot onto the little logs to test them. When he did, he lost his balance.

We had to act now! Now, before he had time to leap back to solid ground—before he knew what was happening.

Every muscle snapped tight as a steel trap. I sucked in a big gulp of air and screamed:

"Now!"

At the very same instant, Jake and I sat up. We grabbed the pole that we had put between us.

The man heard my scream. He jumped back to solid ground and spun around. He must have seen us explode from our hiding place beneath the dirt, because although his face was still hidden in shadow, I could see the whites of his eyes flash wide.

He was too late, though.

Before he could move—before he could even raise the rifle in his hand—Jake and I swung the log. We used it like a battering ram. Aiming it right at the middle of his stomach, we lunged forward with all our might.

He screamed. He flailed his arms, trying to keep his balance. When he did, his rifle went flying far out into the quicksand. He tried to grab the log we had jabbed him with. We yanked it back and rammed it into his stomach again.

With another scream and his arms still spinning around like the blades of a helicopter, he fell backward into the quicksand.

Jake and I leaped to our feet. Still holding the log between us, we rushed to the edge of the quicksand.

The man was grabbing for anything he could get hold of. The small logs we had put at the edge of the quicksand wouldn't hold him. Every time he grabbed one of them, it just went under. He tried to get hold of one of the bigger logs, but the more he struggled and tried to reach out for it, the deeper he sank.

His cowboy hat had fallen off and lay beside him, but

he was facing the wrong direction. We still couldn't see his face.

Jake pulled at my arm. "Let's get out of here!" he screamed. "Let's get his canoe! Come on!"

The dawn light was brighter now. The cowboy hat no longer shielded his face. Finally, the man twisted and turned enough so I could see his face.

"It's Kenny Grissam," I gasped.

CHAPTER 26

We ran for the canoe. At the edge of the shallows, we paused just long enough to make sure there were no alligators. Jake charged across to the island.

I stopped.

The screams stopped me. They haunted me. I turned and looked back at Quicksand Swamp.

"Help me!" he screamed over and over. "Please don't let me die like this. Help me! Please, help me."

"Come on, Ben." Jake motioned for me to follow.

I looked at him, then back at the swamp. I could remember how *I* felt when that sand was pulling me down. I could remember the look on Jake's face—that look of helplessness and panic and fear as the quicksand pulled him deeper and deeper. And I remember what he said to me when he thought he was going to die:

"Tell my daddy I love him."

I looked back at Kenny Grissam. And, as much as I wanted to leave him, as much as he deserved to die a slow, miserable death in that quicksand—I couldn't leave him there.

I went back.

"Help me. Please!" Kenny pleaded. "Don't let me die."

I picked up the log Jake and I had used to knock him into the quicksand. From the island, I could hear Jake screaming at me.

"Don't do it, Ben. You get him out, he'll kill us. Ben! He'll throw us in the quicksand. He'll feed us to the alligators. Ben . . ."

I knew Jake was right. Still . . .

Kenny Grissam had sunk so just his head and shoulders were above the quicksand. His eyes were filled with terror.

I shoved the log toward him.

He grabbed it and started pulling.

"Stop!" I ordered. "I'll keep you from drowning in the quicksand, but if you try to get out, so help me, I'll shove the log out and you'll sink like a rock."

He kept pulling.

I started shoving.

As soon as I did, the end of the log he was clinging to began to sink. So did Kenny Grissam. He stopped pulling.

My eyes tightened as I glared at him.

"I mean it. You just hold on. Nothing more."

Kenny Grissam held onto one end of the log—his head and one arm were all that were left above the quicksand. I held onto the other end of the log.

Now what? I thought to myself.

Behind me, I could hear Jake screaming again. "Here. We're over here!"

I ignored him. I stared Kenny Grissam square in the eye.

"Why?"

He didn't answer. I shook the log.

"Why?" I asked again. "Why did you take our boat? Why did you try to get me eaten by those alligators? We never did anything to you. Why . . . ?"

Behind me, Jake was still yelling, "Here. Over here."

I knew he was trying to get me to come with him to the canoe. I knew he wanted to get out of here. I did, too. But I couldn't leave Kenny Grissam—and I wouldn't leave him—not until I knew why he was trying to kill us. So I tried my best to ignore Jake's yelling.

But then another sound came to my ears. It was another voice.

"There they are! On the island!"

I jumped, suddenly realizing Jake wasn't yelling at me but at someone else.

I put one foot on the end of the log so I could feel if Kenny tried to get out of the quicksand. Then I looked around.

There were two boats coming across the pond toward the island. My heart jumped clear up into my throat. I started waving my arms and screaming as Jake was doing:

"Here! We're over here!"

I felt the log wiggle under my foot. Kenny was still trying to pull himself out. I dropped to one knee and acted like I was going to shove the log farther into the quicksand.

"Okay. Okay," he said quickly, "I won't move. I'll stay right here."

The boats were close enough so I could see who was inside. Daddy, Lisa, and the game ranger were in the first boat. Theodore Grissam, the sheriff, and Jake's dad were in the second. I waved my arms and jumped up and down some more.

It was all I could do to keep from running across to the island to greet them. I wanted to laugh and cry and hug my daddy and hug Lisa and hug Jake's daddy, and even hug the sheriff—only, I stayed right where I was.

I waited.

When they finally reached the island, they all jumped out of their boats and rushed to Jake. They clumped around him and hugged him. I could hear them talking, but I couldn't make out what they were saying. They hugged him some more. Then I could see him pointing at the alligators and the whole mob of people started toward me.

It was then that I dropped down on my knees. I looked Kenny Grissam square in the eye again and started pushing the log.

"What are you doin'?" he screamed. "Don't shove me out. Are you crazy?"

I smiled, never taking my eyes from him.

"Maybe," I said. "Maybe being left out here as alligator bait drove me nuts. Maybe being eaten alive by mosquitoes or gagging at the stench of rotten alligator just drove me crazy. Maybe half starving and being terrified by someone coming in the night to see if we were dead—maybe that drove me clear out of my mind."

His fingernails dug into the log.

"Don't!" he squalled. "I'll die. Don't push it any farther. . . ."

"There will be some people here in a minute," I told him. My voice was so calm and soft, it almost scared *me*. "You're gonna tell all of us why you tried to kill Jake and me. You understand?"

Kenny nodded.

"I've just barely got hold of the end of this log. You tell the truth, and I'll let them pull you in. You lie or decide you don't want to talk"—I shook the log—"all I have to do is give one little shove and you'll be so far out and so deep, nobody will be able to save you. Understand?"

Kenny Grissam nodded.

Daddy was the first to reach me. But just before he got close enough to swoop me up in his arms, I yelled at the top of my lungs:

"*Stop!!!*"

My voice was as loud as my daddy's. It startled me as much as it did him, and he stopped dead in his tracks.

Theodore Grissam was right behind Daddy. He stopped, then when he saw his brother in the quicksand, he started to come closer.

"*Stop!!*" I barked again. "Anybody comes any closer and I'll let go. You'll never see Kenny Grissam again!"

"Ben?" Daddy pleaded. "What's wrong with you, boy? Come here. I've been so worried . . . we thought we'd never see you again. . . . Ben . . . Ben?"

"I mean it," my voice cracked. I fought back my tears. Then with a determination I didn't even know I had, I glared straight into Kenny Grissam's eyes.

"You tell 'em," I growled. "You tell 'em why you wanted me and Jake dead."

His eyes left mine. They seemed to focus on the end of the log that I had, just barely balanced and ready to push into the quicksand.

"It was Robert," he began softly. "I didn't mean for it to be him. It was an accident, really . . . but . . . but . . . I knew if anybody ever found out I killed him . . . they'd send me to jail . . . and . . ."

"Robert," I heard Theodore Grissam gasp behind me. "You know something about Robert? What happened to him? What happened to my boy?"

Kenny Grissam looked up at his brother. "I didn't mean it, Ted," he pleaded. "It was an accident. You've got to believe me. I never meant for Robert to die. . . . Besides, it wasn't me, it was the alligators."

I could see Theodore Grissam out of the corner of my eye when he moved up beside me. I looked back at Kenny and jiggled the end of the log. Kenny's eyes flashed at me. "Start at the beginning," I told him. "Where did the alligators come from?"

Kenny looked at his brother, then back at me. I jiggled the log again.

"Okay. Okay!" he yelped. "I got the alligators a long, long time ago. It was illegal to kill the things, but their hides were worth a lot of money, so I built the fence and kept them here. I fed them. When they'd get big enough, I'd kill them and sell the hides."

Theodore was standing right next to me. "The

boots?" he growled. "The boots you always gave me for Christmas presents . . .?"

Kenny nodded. "They were from the hides of these alligators."

Theodore Grissam dropped to his knees beside me. He tried to shove me out of the way and take the end of the log. I hung on.

"What happened to Robert? Tell me about my boy!"

Theodore Grissam and I were both holding onto the end of the log. Kenny clung desperately to the other end. He swallowed.

"It started when our daddy was dying of cancer," he began. "I knew our old man was going to leave the bank to you. You were always his favorite. No matter how hard I tried . . . no matter how hard I worked . . . you were always Daddy's favorite."

Theodore shook the log.

"Robert. I want to know what happened to Robert."

Kenny glared at him. "It was you," he snarled. "I decided to set a trap for you. With you out of the way, I could get the bank. I could live in the big house. I could be the big shot.

"You were always the adventurous one, always the one who went looking for new places—for excitement. I made up this treasure map. Then I hid it in that old gun I gave you for a birthday present. I knew when you cleaned it up to add it to your gun collection, you'd find the map and come here to search for the treasure. I'd steal your boat and let the alligators . . . they'd . . ."

A tear squeezed from one of Kenny's eyes and left a trail in his quicksand-stained cheek.

"I watched your house for days. I waited for you to take your boat and go looking for the treasure. The second I found your boat missing, I came here. The boat was on the island. I dragged it across the water and tied it in some bushes, then hid in the swamp and waited. . . ."

My eyes tightened. "Just like you did with Jake and me," I breathed.

"But it wasn't you," Kenny went on. "It was Robert. He started swimming for the boat. Before I could get out of my hiding place and get to him . . . before I could get to him . . . the alligator . . . well . . . it . . ." More tears streamed down his cheeks. "I just wanted to be president of the bank. I never meant for Robert . . ."

He broke off and started crying.

"But why us?" I asked. "Why Jake and me?"

Kenny bit his lips together.

"You found the boat. I knew if anyone ever found it, they might figure out what happened. I took it way upstream. That way, if anyone ever did find it, they'd think Robert drowned. They'd never search for him in Quicksand Swamp. Only, when this drought came, the river went down. It washed the dirt and sand away from the bow of the boat and you boys found it."

"You're the one who buried it after I found it," I heard Jake say from behind me. "You sank it once, to hide it, then four years later, when I found it, you tried to hide it again."

Kenny nodded. "I never did find the map I'd made. But you must have, because right after you discovered the boat, you came here. I knew that sooner or later, someone would recognize the boat or you'd show the map or tell about the alligators—something that would make somebody start putting two and two together. I didn't want to go to jail. The only way to be safe was . . . well . . . if no one ever saw you or the boat . . . ever again . . . I'm sorry. I didn't want to hurt you—not really. I'm so sorry."

Theodore let go of the log. He crawled on his hands and knees until he was a few feet away. Then he put his head down against his knees and started to cry. I don't know whether he was crying about his son or for shame about what his brother had done. But he cried and cried.

I felt kind of sad for him. I even felt a little sad for Kenny. I sighed and looked back over my shoulder at Daddy and the sheriff. With a jerk of my head I motioned them to come and get the end of the log so they could drag Kenny Grissam out of the quicksand. When the game ranger and the sheriff came to get him, I rushed to my daddy.

He swooped me up in his arms and hugged me so hard I thought my eyes were going to pop clear out of my head. I didn't mind, though. In fact, it felt awful good. He kissed me about a hundred times. That felt good, too.

When he let me go, I picked Lisa up and hugged and kissed her.

"I told them where to find you," she said. "I tried to tell them for two days, but that mean ol' Kenny told everybody that he saw your boat at Jacob's Bend, so nobody would listen to me."

I kissed her and held her out at arm's length. "Just how did you know where to find us?"

"I had seen the map," she said, smiling. "I found it in the old tree the day I found the cork doll."

Daddy came up and hugged both of us. "She did try to tell us," he said. "We took her over to stay with Tiffany while we searched at Jacob's Bend. She took the cork doll with her. Tiffany and Theodore saw it and recognized it as one that Robert had made for his little sister. Then we listened."

"Grown-ups don't ever listen to little kids," she grumped.

Daddy hugged us again. We laughed and cried and kissed and hugged. Then we went home.

* * *

Kenny Grissam didn't have much of a trial. Jake and I didn't even have to go to court to repeat what he had told us, because he pleaded guilty to the murder of Robert Grissam and they sent him to jail.

Theodore Grissam gave us the reward money, as it said on the posters all over Broken Bow. But for some reason, we didn't go buy the boat that we'd always talked about. The way we felt, we really didn't need a boat. Fishing from the hard, solid ground at the bank seemed good enough for us. So when Grandma suggested that we leave it in a savings account in the bank and use it for college someday, we agreed.

Jake and I did take enough out to buy Lisa a couple of new dolls. Jake got her one with batteries. It crawls and cries and wets in its pants. I got her a pretty china doll with lace all over. She still likes her little cork doll the best, though.

Jake and I like it, too. If Lisa hadn't been snooping around in our hiding place and found it and the map, Jake and I might still be stuck on that island— surrounded by mosquitoes and alligators and quicksand. For some reason, having my little sister prowl around in my stuff doesn't bother me anymore.

ABOUT THE AUTHOR

BILL WALLACE lives outside Chickasha, Oklahoma, on a farm, where he has five dogs, three cats, and two horses. When not answering letters from children, spending time with his wife, children, and grandchildren, he works on his books. *Beauty; Ferret in the Bedroom, Lizards in the Fridge* (winner of the Nebraska Golden Sower Award and the South Carolina Children's Book Award); *Danger at Panther Peak* (original title: *Shadow on the Snow*); *Danger in Quicksand Swamp* and Snot Stew are available in Minstrel Books. *A Dog Called Kitty* (winner of the Nebraska Golden Sower Award, the Oklahoma Sequoyah Award, and the Texas Bluebonnet Award), *Trapped in Death Cave* (winner of the Utah Children's Book Award), and *Red Dog* are available in Archway Paperbacks.